Making Sense

Nadia Marks was born in Cyprus, but grew up in North London, where she now lives with her husband and two sons. An ex-creative director on a number of leading women's magazines, she now works as a freelance journalist for several national newspapers and magazines.

Making Sense

by Nadia Marks

Piccadilly Press • London

First published in Great Britain in 2003
by Piccadilly Press Ltd,
5 Castle Road, London NW1 8PR

A catalogue record for this book is available from the British Library

ISBN: 1 85340 748 8 (trade paperback)

1 3 5 7 9 10 8 6 4 2

Printed and bound in Great Britain by Bookmarque Ltd
Typeset by Textype Typesetters
Cover design by Fielding Design
Set in Goudy

For my beloved mother and father,
who gave me everything.

And for all who in their different ways played a part
in this book, I thank you.
Graham, who made it possible and believed in me.
My sons, Leo and Pablo, who are carrying on their
Cypriot culture. For my brother, Yianni, and almost-brother,
Tony, who both taught me so much. Soula, who will always
be in my heart, and Magdalena, for her beautiful eyes.
Loukis, Maro, my auntie Eleni and my grandfather Hadji-
Lucas, for my wonderful childhood memories. Christina,
who never judges me, Athenoula for loving me, and Cyprus,
for just being there. Francie, Linda and Gill, who showed me
another culture, and Trudy, Liliana, Yuriko, Alison, Linda B
and Pamela, who all know what it's like to be an outsider.

Thank you to Brenda, my publisher, for asking me to
write this book, and Yasemin, my editor, for all her
help and valid comments.

CHAPTER ONE

Culture Shock

'My friend wants to shag your brother,' one of the two big girls in the playground tells me. She is standing very close and looking at me with grey-blue eyes and an expression I cannot read. Her arm is linked with her friend's, a black girl, who is chewing gum and has her head tilted to one side, wearing an equally baffling expression.

Those are probably the first English words I understand at the comprehensive school my seventeen-year-old brother Tony and I are sent to when we first arrive in England. I'm rooted to the ground, unable to respond, simply because I have no language to respond in. I speak no English, apart from a few words, which are to say I don't understand. Stella, the friend I've been walking around with during our break, starts to giggle and I know from her expression that something rude has just been said. I'm familiar with the sound of the word 'shag' – I've heard it used a lot in the playground.

Stella's a Greek Cypriot like me, but she's been in England for about seven or eight months, so she has a lot more words in her vocabulary and she can string them together. When we eventually walk away from the girls, she translates.

I don't know whether to be insulted, or to be proud that I have such a desirable brother, but one thing is for sure – I'm shocked at the blatant way the girls expressed themselves. Where I come from, even if you were madly in love, you wouldn't dream of letting a boy know how you felt in such a shameless way. You might hold hands with him or let him kiss you at a party, but shagging was definitely not in the picture.

'Julia,' I hear Christina, one of the other Greek girls from our class, shouting at me as she runs towards us from across the playground, 'what did those big girls want with you?' she asks. The kids in my class, which was especially created to help immigrant children learn English, keep well away from the other kids in the playground – partly because most of us can't understand what they're saying and partly because we find them a bit scary.

'They want to sleep with her big brother,' Stella informs her.

'Well, he is a bit good-looking,' Christina says, and we fall about laughing.

Our class is a collection of Cypriot (both Greek and Turkish), Asian, Somalian and Eastern European kids – and one Chinese girl. Anarchy rules, but in a good-humoured way, because no one is rude or aggressive. It's just that none of us speak English, so we talk to each other in our native tongues – apart from the Chinese girl, because she has no one else from her country to talk to. Our teacher, Miss Appleyard, whose name we all giggled at when we discovered what it meant, does her best to make us talk to each other in English, but frankly, she doesn't succeed.

Up until the time I arrived in England with my parents and brother, only three months ago, I knew exactly who I was. Ioulia Lemonides, fourteen years old, confident, popular, artistic and lively. Since we arrived in London on that cold, dull August day from our hot Mediterranean island, I've been in a state of shock and totally confused about my identity. As if it wasn't enough that no one could pronounce my surname and everybody kept calling me 'Lemonade', no one could get their mouth round my first name either. So I had to change it to Julia, which meant that most of the time, when people called me, I ignored them. It feels like I'm in a trance, or a bad dream that I can't wake up from. The playground is dull and grey, the school, an ancient red brick building, is huge and impersonal – a labyrinth of a place and so easy to get lost in. Unable to communicate with anyone apart from the other Greek kids to find out how to get from room to room, I stick very closely to Stella.

'So, are you going to tell your brother about this?' asks Christina.

'He doesn't care. He thinks they're all stupid and he hates this school anyway,' I say as we walk around the noisy playground.

My brother, who is handsome in a dark, brooding kind of way, is far more sophisticated and grown-up looking than any of the other kids his age. He appears really cool, which he is – but his aloofness and moody silence is more

3

to do with the fact that, although he speaks English, he's by no means fluent, and he too is lost and confused in this new environment we have both been thrown into.

My parents chose this particular school because it had a sixth form, so the two of us would be together. But, although my brother is here, I still feel terrified most of the time. I'm used to a nice, friendly school in a small town, on a small island, where I know everybody. Now I'm in a massive building in the middle of one of the biggest cities in the world, the likes of which I've never seen before in all my life, with thousands of strangers. And to top it all off, I don't understand a word anyone says to me.

'It will be great, you'll see. Nothing to worry about,' my dad said to me before we left Cyprus, 'and your big brother will be there to look after you.'

Yeah, right, I thought. He would be there and he'd take me on the bus with him to school, but I knew my brother – he would dump me the moment he could and I would be on my own. I was fourteen and he was very nearly eighteen, but looked twenty-five – he didn't want *me* around. His little sister was the biggest pain in his life and he was lumbered with me. In Cyprus he could give me a wide berth and our paths didn't have to meet. But now, in London, we are all cooped up together and in each other's faces all the time.

CHAPTER TWO

Uprooted

'How would you like to go to England?' my mother asked me cheerfully one day while she was laying the table for lunch. I'd just walked through the kitchen door from school. I was back for the midday break and soon my dad and brother would be home too so we could all have lunch together, like all Cypriot families.

'A lot! Why?' I replied, as I put down my satchel, grabbed a piece of crunchy celery and sat down at the kitchen table. I looked at her quizzically and waited for her to explain. We had never been abroad before, so her question was unexpected. I couldn't quite believe it. London! The centre of fashion, pop music and movie stars – was she teasing me?

'When?' I added excitedly before she could say any more.

'In August,' she said, and then in an everyday voice, as if it was the most natural thing in the world, she added, 'We're all going to go and live there for a few years.'

Her words didn't compute. I stared at her face, expecting to see her break into a big smile to let me know she was joking.

'Oh, yeah, right,' I said, attempting to smile. 'Just like that!' The smile was fading away from my lips. 'Mama! You *are* joking . . . ?' I continued, my voice a little shaky by now.

'No, no,' my mum replied in the same cheerful voice. 'It's true – it's your dad's job. He's been asked to go to England.'

The food my mother had cooked smelled wonderful on that warm spring day. The windows and kitchen door were both open, bringing the sunshine and the fragrant smells of the garden into the house, creating a delicious blend of flowers and cooking. Suddenly, I felt dizzy and nauseous. My mum looked up and saw the colour had drained from my face.

'What's the matter?' she asked.

'I don't feel so well,' I told her, tears welling up in my eyes, as I ran out to the garden, where my cat, Chloe, was sleeping luxuriously in the sunshine. I sat next to her and touched her warm fur. She automatically rewarded me with her loudest purr. My mother's words were still echoing in my head. I couldn't believe what she'd just said. What did she mean we were going to go and live in England? No discussions, nothing! What about me? I didn't want to go and live there! I wanted to go to London to be a tourist and see the sights and buy clothes and records, and then come home and show off to my friends. Why would I want to live there? I have never even been there. I have never been anywhere! My eyes blurred with overflowing tears as I bent down to pick up Chloe and squeezed her tight in my arms. I'd had her for three years, ever since I found her in the gutter on my way home from school one day. She was just a few weeks old and nearly dead, but I nursed her back to health, so she loved me and I loved her, and I knew I would never be able to take her with me if I had to leave.

Chloe was not the only thing I would have to leave behind, and the thought made me shudder. It seemed so crazy to be leaving just as things were finally getting back to normal for us after the war of two summers ago. I wouldn't have minded going then like other people did, but now it seemed stupid.

After a little while, worried about my sudden outburst, Mum came out into the garden and put her arms around me, trying to comfort me.

'I'm sorry, Ioulia *mou*,' she said. ('*Mou*' is a term of endearment in Greek; it means 'mine'.) 'I should have realised it would have been a bit of a shock for you. I really didn't think you'd react like this. I thought you'd be excited. We will talk about it with your dad and Tony over lunch. It's going to be just fine, just wait and see.'

Over lunch, my dad explained that he had a job opportunity that would require him to work in London for a few years, and that going to live in England as a family for a while would be a good thing for everyone. Now that stability was back in our country, it would be fine to leave for a few years, knowing that we could come back and our house would be safe, and everything would be fine. My brother would go to University and both of us would have the opportunity for a British education, which was brilliant.

I looked at Tony for signs of how he was feeling about all this, but as always he was giving nothing away. He just carried on eating in his usual way, cool and grown-up about everything. I should have known that I was the last person he would share his feelings with, even if he was worried or upset about leaving. But what about all his friends? He had a fantastic crowd of school friends – mostly really good-looking boys that my friends and I would drool over. But there were a few girls too. Especially Maria, who I knew was special because I'd seen them kissing one evening in the garden behind the pomegranate tree. Wouldn't he miss her? Why wasn't he telling them that they couldn't just do this without asking us.

'You will go to an English school and learn to speak English like an English girl!' Dad continued enthusiastically, looking at me with pride. 'Isn't that going to be something?'

'How does it feel not understanding anything people say?' wrote my beloved cousin Sophia, a few weeks after we moved to London. I miss her more than anyone. Sophia and I were as close as you can get – we were practically attached at the hip. Although she had two older sisters and I had my brother, we did everything together from a very young age and loved each other like sisters. 'If you die I will kill myself!' we used to pledge to each other. During the summer of the invasion, when our two families and other friends and neighbours moved in together for support, Sophia and I spent most of our time clinging to each other. My departure to England was a heavy blow to both of us.

'It feels like being deaf and dumb,' I wrote back. 'Unbearably lonely.'

Stella and the other Greek girls at school are no substitute for Sophia, but at least with their limited knowledge of English, they are some kind of link to the small universe of the school playground.

CHAPTER THREE

Adjusting

'I'm giving up with the lot of you!' shouts the usually docile Miss Appleyard as we all continue to ignore her and talk amongst ourselves in our own languages. Stella is in the middle of telling all the other Greek kids about the incident in the playground, and the boys are particularly interested in this.

'Did they actually say shag?' asks Costas, a fourteen-year-old Cypriot boy with bushy eyebrows and a moustache that makes him look like he's got a charcoal smudge on his upper lip. 'Do you think she might want to shag *me?*'

Stella laughs at him. 'You must be joking! You're not exactly Tony, are you? You don't even speak English and she's a foot taller than you!'

'Well, I don't care. I could teach her a few things, because I did it with a twenty-five-year-old woman from my village last summer, just before we came here, and she really liked it,' Costas says, smiling boastfully.

'She must have been the village idiot,' Stella replies.

'Just because you fancy Tony and he doesn't even

know you exist . . .' Costas hits back at her.

'Will you lot just shut up!' shouts our teacher. 'I don't know what you're talking about, but if you carry on this noise I will get the headmaster!'

All my friends, ever since I can remember, fall in love with Tony. I don't know why – he just ignores them all. He never says a word to any of them and treats us all like pests. I suppose girls just like the handsome, silent type. I know Stella likes Tony and she thinks that by hanging around with me and coming to our house after school she might get him to notice her. What I don't tell her is that Tony likes women, not girls, and preferably women over twenty who are at university or have left school and are working. He doesn't have a girlfriend yet, but I can see the way he looks at the more sophisticated types on the bus and tube. Anyone wearing a uniform is invisible to him. Stella has no chance, but I don't tell her that either. Right now, she's the only friend I have.

'We can move next week!' Mum says excitedly, smiling from ear to ear as she hangs up the phone.

Here we go again, I think. Moving and starting all over again, just as I'm starting to find my way around. Mum has been desperate to find a new place for us to live ever since we came to London. Although the flat we were given by my dad's company on our arrival is lovely and in a really good area, close to the centre of London and our school, it lacks one essential asset: Greek neighbours. As far as my mother is concerned, these are impossible living conditions. If I have problems with English, my mother's

11

problems are even worse. At least I'm at school learning, and I know it's only a matter of time before I start understanding what is going on around me. She on the other hand, is left at home alone from early morning till we all come back at the end of the day. It is really lonely for her – she is completely isolated. The evening classes she enrolled in at the local adult education centre don't seem to be helping either. But it's the lack of company she misses most.

'I'm just hopeless at this,' she complained. 'I'm terrible at languages and I'm never going to be able to even do the shopping in this country without one of you coming with me.'

The only thing to do, it was decided, was to find some more Greeks and move closer to them for company, which wasn't so difficult, since there are so many Greeks living in London. 'At least then I'll have someone to talk to during the day when you're all out,' she said.

My mum is the most sociable person I know. She loves company. She considers being alone for any period of time a punishment, and can't understand why anyone would be alone by choice. Greeks always come in crowds. They consider it their duty to ensure that no one is ever left alone, even if they want to be. You *never* see a solitary Greek; in fact, the word 'privacy' does not exist in the Greek language. So for my mum, the first few months have been like hell, and I feel sorry for her.

The place my mum has found for us is miles out of the centre of London. It is the last stop on the Northern Line, in a suburb with rows of boring semi-detached houses, but my mum loves it. Tony and I have a long journey to school and it's dark by the time we get home. On the way there I keep very close to him and for once he doesn't seem to mind.

A Cypriot family, who had also moved to England and who my mum knew through one of her friends back home, had bought a small semi-detached house that had a spare kitchen and two bathrooms. They too were desperate for company, so it was decided that the house was perfectly adequate for two families to live in together. We moved into the two upper rooms of the house. Two families crammed into what is basically five rooms! The only good thing that can be said about this arrangement, is that we have company.

The other family are called Seferis, and *Kyria* Eva and *Kyrios* Petros ('*Kyria*' and '*Kyrios*' mean 'Mrs' and 'Mr' in Greek) also have a son, Stavros, and a daughter, Anna. Anna and her brother are both a bit older than me and my brother, but they missed Cyprus and their Cypriot friends as much as we did, so they welcomed the company. They came to England in less fortunate circumstances than us. The invasion of our country by Turkey and the bloody war that followed resulted in the island being partitioned and separated in two. The north became the Turkish part and the south Greek, but if your house happened to be in the wrong part of the island, you had to run for your life. Our new friends were in the wrong part, but luckily they managed to escape to the south, leaving their home and everything they had

13

behind, and then to England, like so many others in their position.

The upper part of the house consists of two rooms, a tiny kitchen and a tiny bathroom. My brother and I have to share a bedroom, something that we haven't done since we were very young (and then it was only on holiday). My parents have to sleep in the living-room on a sofa-bed that has to be put away every morning to make it back into a sitting room/dining room. Not much space for any kind of privacy here!

'People have to put up with much worse conditions than this,' Mum said when both Tony and I started complaining about sharing a room and the lack of space in general. 'At least we are all alive and well and still have each other.'

We knew she was right. We had witnessed war and its aftermath, the loss of lives and people's homes, and thousands of refugees fleeing the island. At least we were doing this for companionship and not for survival.

We've been living with the Seferis family for two weeks now, and the snow started falling the day after we moved in. None of us has ever seen snow before. The spectacle is thrilling. We're oblivious to the fact that it is not *at all* normal. It's only a few days till Christmas and so far it has been the worst winter England has seen for fifty years or something like that!

Everybody is telling us how unusual it is for snow to fall for so many days. The news on the radio and TV is full of talk about the weather, but since we don't know any better, we all assume this is a normal English winter. Before coming over, my grandfather and my auntie Eleni were very worried about how we would cope with the hard winters, and everyone was preparing us for cold and frost, snow and rain, so we were not particularly surprised.

'What do you want to do when you leave school?' Anna asks me as we watch our brothers through the living-room window, making a snowman in the back garden. It's funny seeing our older brothers behave like a couple of excited little boys.

'I want to go to art school,' I say, 'but I can't imagine ever leaving school or ever speaking English well enough to do anything!'

'Don't be silly,' she says. 'By the summer you'll be fine. Look at me.'

Anna, who is two years older, but looks younger than me, is small and very slim, with big brown-green eyes, a turned-up nose and straight, glossy dark hair – a contrast to my masses of brown curls. She is very pretty, in a petite kind of way, and she already spoke English when she came to London. Like Tony, her English was shaky at the beginning and she couldn't communicate that well, but she picked it up quickly and is now fluent. Still, Anna is clever and studious and spends most of her time studying – I can't compare myself to her.

Anna's mum is delighted that finally her daughter has a friend to spend time with. 'Now with Ioulia around, she might take her nose out of those books and do something else,' I hear her say to Mum. 'A girl her age should have some other interests apart from books,' she continues, while my mum is wishing I would do a bit *more* studying and less watching television (which I have discovered is the best way to learn English).

Having a friend on the doorstep is brilliant and I imagine it's a bit like having a sister. Anna is sweet and friendly and our age difference doesn't seem to matter at all. Back home, I would never have expected a girl two years older than me to be my friend, but here in London, we are both grateful for the company.

The only time I get to spend with Stella now we've moved house is at school, and she is still pining for Tony. 'I never see you anymore,' she complains. 'Can't I come and stay at your house over the weekend?'

'You must be joking. We live in a matchbox with a bunch of other people. You'd have to sleep in the same room as me and Tony,' I tell her, feeling embarrassed.

She giggles. 'That would be fine with me.'

'You're just sex-mad,' I tell her. 'You can't imagine how annoying it is to share a room with your brother.'

'I wouldn't mind sharing a room with your brother.'

'You wouldn't fancy him at all if you shared a room with him, I promise. He takes over all the space with his smelly socks and books and records, and he always wakes me up when he comes to bed. He's so bloody noisy and he thinks he's God!'

'Well, as far as I'm concerned, he is,' she says, all dreamy-eyed.

CHAPTER FOUR

Displaced

By Christmas my parents have decided that enough is enough with my school and I have to go to a new one. Miss Appleyard is not able to discipline her class and unless I stop talking in Greek and start seriously learning English, I have no hope of learning anything.

Our first Christmas in England was a total non-event, a truly unmemorable occasion, spent just with our two families and the TV. Anna and I tried to cheer things up by decorating a tree and wrapping all the presents in pretty paper. Our mums cooked a turkey and all the things that go with it, but somehow nothing felt quite right. We were all too homesick. If it weren't for all the fun we had with the snow, things would have been a bit depressing.

My new school is all girls and it's much nearer to home. It is modern and faceless, a concrete block of a building, and totally different to the old red brick school I've just left. I walk part of the way to school with Anna, then she catches her bus and I continue on foot. It's a very different journey to the one I made with Tony by bus and tube, and a world apart from the one I made in my country.

I walk on my own, feeling isolated and lonely, wishing I could join the group of girls from my school who are talking and laughing. Some even walk and chat with boys from the nearby school in the same way I did with my friends in the mixed school I went to in Cyprus. We would pick each other up on the way, joking, laughing and teasing, and make our way to class in a big friendly crowd.

The snow is piled up on the side of the road to clear the pavements, and the greyness of the sky, the cold air and lack of light make me shiver while I walk. The trees along the way have no leaves and their naked branches add to the melancholic mood that hangs heavily in the air. All the trees and plants seem dead.

Even in August when we first arrived, I didn't like English gardens. The first ones I saw were from the train on our way to Victoria station from Dover. Flashing by the window were rows and rows of identical houses and gardens – little patches of green grass and neatly planted flower beds with brightly coloured flowers – and I was filled with a sadness that I couldn't explain. Dad enthused at the marvellous green of the land and the fabulous variety of flowers growing in the parks. 'The rain makes things grow! You can see this is a country with plenty of water!' He said, comparing it to the lack of water our island always suffered from. When we started visiting the city's parks, I realised that light was the key to how everything looked and that when the sun was shining, everything was transformed. The dull English summer light seemed to accentuate the colours around me, but there seemed to be far too much green for my liking – and not a cheerful kind of green, but a dark, sombre colour contrasting with the flowers beds, making them look almost artificial. I would bend over to smell the flowers and smell nothing and think, if the rain makes things grow, then it must be the sun that gives them life.

In Cyprus I used to identify the seasons by the smells of things. Hot summer nights were scented with the sweet smell of jasmine, the aroma of narcissus signalled the start of spring, and in the autumn I would bury my face in the myriad petals of chrysanthemums, covered with early-morning dew, and breathe in their peculiar scent. The winters were filled with the smell of mandarins and oranges and my pockets bulged from the fruits I would pick from the trees in our garden to eat on the way to school. Their smell would linger on my fingers all through the day. In England, I smell almost nothing!

In my new school, the antiquated heating system consists of massive radiators, and Miss Hammond, our English teacher, always asks the girls to move so I can sit beside the one in our classroom during lessons because she feels sorry for me.

'Let Julia sit by the heating. She comes from a hot country and she is not used to this cold,' she says. I don't think this is doing anything for my popularity. The girls found me interesting at first, a novelty, but now, what with Miss Hammond being so nice to me, I'm not sure what they think.

Miss Hammond is a pretty, round-faced young woman with the straightest blond hair I have ever seen. It hangs down to her shoulders all around her face like a curtain, and when the girls are being particularly rude to her, she flushes bright red and hides behind it. I think she is really sweet and gentle and I know she finds some of the girls hard to take. I saw her eyes fill up once. I sit silently, watching my classmates' behaviour and gasp sometimes at their rudeness. In Cyprus, we would never have dreamed of treating any of our teachers with such disrespect.

Lessons are a strange affair too, because after the teachers finish giving the other girls work, they take me to one side and we just work on English. It's really helpful, because I'm beginning to understand a few more words. However, I feel the other girls' eyes on me and they obviously think I'm lucky because I'm not working like they are. They must think it's easy! I really want to scream and tell them that's rubbish and that all I want is to be like them and be able to talk and understand and be normal. Instead, I sit patiently, working and waiting, and try to make sense of everything going on around me.

CHAPTER FIVE

A Soul Mate

The cold air hits our warm faces as Anna and I come out into the garden to look at another snowman the boys have made. It's been snowing on and off for so long now and there is so much of it that this snowman is as big as a man and ten times better than the first one the boys made.

Suddenly, a torrent of snowballs thrown by Tony and Stavros bombard us, taking our breath away, and we hit back at them with shrieks and laughter. A full-blown snow fight breaks out between us, the likes of which we've only ever seen in the movies, and although I'm bitterly cold and wearing more clothes than is comfortable, it's really exhilarating. Our faces are flushed and our noses are running, but it's such fun, and so nice that our big brothers are finally taking some notice of us – even if we are just targets for snowballs!

We have snow in Cyprus, but only in the mountains during the winter months, and although it was only a few hours drive to the snowy peaks, we never went there, no matter how much I begged my parents. Due to Dad's work,

Mum was forced to spend a large part of her early married life, when my brother was a baby, travelling around and living in primitive conditions in different mountain villages, so she would only go back in the summer. The idea of winter in the mountains made her shiver and she would lift her arms up in horror and say, 'Why on earth would we want to go there? It's freezing!' So, it was in England that I first saw snowflakes fall and settle on the ground like a thick, fluffy cotton-wool carpet. And I love it! Everyone else moans about it, but if you've never seen it before, it's brilliant and on top of that, the heating at my new school never works properly, so we have days off, like today, which is even better!

'You're so lucky having days off school,' Anna says as she's getting ready to leave for the day.

'Why don't you pretend you're ill and stay at home with me, then?' I suggest. Anna is very conscientious and takes school seriously. She plans to go to university, preferably Oxford, so she is working very hard for her exams. However, my suggestion proves too tempting. When she opens the door and sees the snow falling like a thick white veil, she says, 'Wait here,' and puts her bag down with a wicked smile. 'I'll be back in a minute.'

She returns a few moments later, and as she takes off her coat, scarf, gloves and woolly hat, one by one, I wonder what she's said to her mother to convince her to let her stay.

'I just told her that my throat was killing me every time I swallowed, which means we'll be having soup and hot drinks all day, but it's worth it!' she says and we both start laughing.

The house is warm and cozy, and we have it all to ourselves, since both our mothers have ventured out to the supermarket, which is a real performance for them in these weather conditions. Anyone would think they were heading for the North Pole, dressed like a couple of yetis with shopping bags. We laughed so much as we watched them stagger down the street.

We are alone for a couple of hours and we decide that the best thing to do is indulge in our favourite pastime of putting on make-up. We love make-up and we are trying to learn as much as we can about how to wear it by constantly flipping through magazines and practising. Anna is hopeless, but I, on the other hand, have a pretty good idea of how to apply it, because it's just like drawing, which is what I do best. It is my passion and whenever I have a spare moment to myself, I love to draw. I'm happiest when I'm sketching and I want to go to art school to study fashion design.

'Come on, then, let's get the make-up out,' I tell her, 'I'll do your eyes today.' We are on a mission at the moment because we are planning a whole day's shopping trip in the West End and want to look our best. Mum agreed to let me go with Anna since she's older and speaks English, but it took a lot of convincing. We've been spending almost every evening and Saturday morning locked in Anna's bedroom, practising. I read in a magazine that when you go shopping you should always look perfect, otherwise nothing looks good on you. We have decided on next Saturday for our outing, so we don't have much time left. Anna's big almond-shaped eyes, with their long eyelashes, are great for making up, so by the time I've finished applying eyeshadow, lots of mascara and a bit of black kohl, she looked like a model.

'I read in a Greek magazine that you have to either emphasise the eyes or the lips. You can't do both or you look cheap.' I tell her.

'I suppose it's a bit like you either wear a short skirt or a plunging neckline. It's either legs or boobs, and since I have no boobs, it's going to have to be legs and eyes for me,' Anna replies and we both fall about laughing.

'Yeah, but I *do* have boobs,' I say, 'so is it going to be lips and boobs for me?'

'Well, I suppose it would be a good thing if we didn't look the same – that way we both have something different to offer,' she says, giggling.

'Don't know who we are offering it too, since neither of us have a boyfriend!'

'People look,' says Anna. 'At least they can look at two different types.'

'That's true, but it would be nice to have a boyfriend or at least someone we could flirt with a bit.'

'I know! But you're only fourteen – you've got plenty of time. Look at me – I'm sixteen and the closest I got to a boyfriend was last summer at that beach party when that creep tried to stick his tongue down my throat! Yuck!'

'I suppose if you had liked him you wouldn't have minded,' I tell her. 'Some of the girls in my class have boyfriends. I see them walking together after school and

I'm sure what they get up to is more than tongues down throats . . .'

'Don't you believe it – most of them are just showing off,' says Anna, checking her eye make-up in the mirror. 'They're always boasting about it in my school as well, but I'm sure half of them don't know any more than us.'

'I suppose you're right, and to tell you the truth, since I can't understand what they're saying, I'm only guessing. It's all in their body language, though. They seem to know so much!' I sigh. 'I just don't know if I like this new school.'

'At least you don't have to go on hundreds of buses and trains to get there now,' Anna says, pointing out the positive side of things as usual, while rummaging through her wardrobe.

'I know, but it's so boring with no boys. You don't have to speak to boys – you just look at them, but with girls you need to talk to make friends and sometimes they seem bitchy. I just don't know how I'm ever going to make any friends there.'

The girls at my new school are a real mixed bunch. Some seem nice, but some are really tough and pretty aggressive. The school itself is OK, but the trouble is, I'm not used to being with only girls. I feel strange there, like a real outsider, and the girls just don't seem to be as friendly as in the old school. Well, I say that, but the friends I had at the old school were Greek kids. At my new school, I'm the only foreign girl – or at least the only one who doesn't speak English, so I stand out like a sore thumb and feel like a freak.

'OK. What about this?' she says, picking out a tartan mini-skirt. 'With my lace-up boots and my black polo-neck jumper?' she asks.

'Great! All legs and eyes!'

'What are you going to wear?

'Jeans and red lips!' I say. 'But I'm going to freeze to death if I put on a low-cut top.'

'You can wear your zip-up red jumper to go with your lips and you can leave it open a bit or zip it up if it gets too cold,' she says as she slips into her skirt for a trial run.

'Soup's ready!' *Kyria* Eva calls up to us. They must have been back for ages, but we've been so wrapped up in what we're doing that we didn't hear a thing.

'And about time too,' Anna says, giggling. 'My throat is killing me.'

CHAPTER SIX

Wrong Turn

'You've got to be back by five,' both sets of parents agree as we are getting ready for our big day out in the centre of London.

'It gets dark by four o'clock, so you mustn't be late,' Dad says. 'Call us from the tube station and we'll pick you up.'

We are dressed up and ready to leave, all big eyes and red lips, when my brother Tony walks into the house. He stares, speechless, at Anna and me, in what I can only describe as amazement.

'You can't be serious,' he says to Mum. 'You're not letting them go out looking like that, are you?'

'Why? What's wrong with them?' our mothers reply in unison.

'They look about twenty-five, that's what's wrong with them,' he says, horrified. 'Don't you realise? This is asking for trouble, letting them go around looking like that. No one is going to believe they are a couple of little girls.'

'They're hardly little girls,' Mum says. 'They're teenagers

27

and they are sensible young ladies, so leave them alone,' she says in our defence.

As offended as we are by his sexist remarks, we are also feeling pretty flattered that the almighty Tony thinks we look that good.

'Well, just be careful, you two, and don't talk to anyone,' he says and walks off in his usual moody way.

As we make our way to the station, we are both beaming with delight. If Tony thinks we could cause a stir, then we *must* look good. He has such high standards. Anna is especially pleased because I know, even if she hasn't said anything, she too has fallen under the spell of my 'gorgeous' brother.

The bright sunlight is almost blinding as we come out of the underground at Oxford Circus. It's a cold sunny day, under a clear, cloudless blue sky, and the snow has melted here – a total contrast to the suburbs, where the pavements are still covered. The January sales are still on and the shops are bursting with fabulous things. We hardly know where to start.

There is visual noise from the myriad things to look at, and our ears are buzzing from the traffic, the music blaring from the shops, and the crowds of people bustling around. The two famous streets – Oxford Street and Regent Street – that I've heard so much about, are here, stretching ahead of us and beckoning us to 'shop till we drop'. It is so fantastic! We both feel so free and grown-up and independent.

We walk past the Dickens and Jones department store

and I'm reminded of the last time I was there, soon after we arrived in England. I went shopping with my mum and one of her friends who was visiting us for a few days from Cyprus. Her English was marginally better than my mum's, which meant that she knew about seven words rather than three. The two of them insisted on engaging the sales assistant in an incomprehensible discussion about a bargain for a winter coat. My aunt had asked my mother to buy one and send it back with the visiting friend. Obviously bargaining is something that is done naturally in our country, but this was Regent Street! Oh my God! It was so embarrassing that I had to hide behind a pillar and pretend I didn't know either of them. I start telling Anna about it and the memory makes me flush with embarrassment.

'How humiliating! You poor thing. What the hell did they say to the sales woman?' she asks, cringing at the mere thought. 'Were they talking to her in Greek?'

'I have no idea,' I tell her. 'I couldn't bare it beyond the first few seconds. I just hid and left them to it.'

'What happened in the end?'

'All I can tell you is that, miraculously, they bought the coat and got it at a reduced price. It turns out that apparently you *can* bargain. I think you have to be a Greek or an Arab to even think about doing such a thing, but there you go. Frankly, I'd rather die.'

Laughing and joking, arms linked through each other's, we walk in and out of shops, trying on clothes, shoes, bags, hats, and everything that takes our fancy. We are so excited and happy and having the best day so far since we've been in London. This is what I imagined in the brief moments after my mum first told me the news about coming to England, when I thought it was just going to be a holiday. As the thought flashes through my mind, it makes me smile, and for the first time I can see some of the advantages of living in London. What an incredible difference five months can make.

'Shall we stop for a drink and a sandwich?' Anna suggests and we come across a nice coffee bar on a side street, with lots of people in it. Our mothers made us promise we would stop and have something to eat. The place we choose feels so sophisticated and grown-up and we wallow in the sheer pleasure of being in the middle of the metropolis, amongst all the Londoners having lunch or afternoon tea. I looked around at men and women, fashionably dressed with shopping bags, couples sitting close together talking in hushed voices, out on a date, and waiters buzzing about taking orders. It is brilliant! We find a booth, take our coats off and spread ourselves out. Anna suggests I undo the zip of my red jumper just a little for the desired look. We check each other out and we both agree we look just like any English girls out shopping.

We are just about finishing off our club sandwiches and Cokes when two guys who look like students ask if they can join us. Before Anna has a chance to say anything, they sit down. They look about nineteen or twenty and one of them is holding a huge maroon-coloured folder, which I recognise as an art portfolio. I think I hear them saying 'I hope you don't mind' to Anna, and then something else I don't understand. She smiles and says, 'No.'

'They want to sit here because the place is too full,' she translates for me.

'I suppose it's OK,' I reply. 'I think one of them is an art student.'

'How do you know?' she asks.

'He looks very arty and he's got a portfolio. If they talk to us again will you ask him?'

'Where are you from?' asks the art student, looking at me with piercing blue eyes and I understand perfectly because it's one of the first sentences I learned.

'From Cyprus,' I say, blushing, and looking at Anna in a panic in case he asks me more. Anna explains that I don't speak much English and that we've only been in England a few months and a conversation starts up between the four of us. It turns out that I was right – the guys, Tom and Peter, are students, one studying Art and the other Law. They buy us coffee and ask a lot of questions, and Anna translates. We all laugh a lot and they ask for our phone numbers. They obviously think we are older, or at least that I am. I know they would die if they knew I was only fourteen.

Suddenly I look at my watch and I break out in a cold sweat. It's half past four. We had strict instructions to be back by five and the journey by tube is an hour long – and that's from the station.

'Oh my God!' I hiss at Anna, who is deep in conversation with the Law student about the political situation in Cyprus.

31

'What's wrong?' she says, startled.

'Look at your watch,' I tell her and feel grateful that we are talking in Greek. How can we tell these boys that we have to rush home or our parents will kill us. It seems so strange and backward and I'm sure that's not what English girls do.

Anna tells them we have to go and they seem disappointed. We gather our bags and coats and dash out.

'I gave him my phone number,' Anna tells me as we are leaving the coffee bar. 'I've never done that before. Maybe I should have taken his number instead,' she says, a bit worried.

'Too late now,' I reply as we step onto the pavement.

Once we're out we realise that it has suddenly gone dark – we'd walked into the bar in bright daylight and came out in darkness. How could night have fallen in just a couple of hours?

Everything looks completely different at night, and the little side street gives us no signs of which way to walk to get to the underground station. What looked familiar one minute now looks completely different and a bit scary.

'I'm sure it's this way,' says Anna and we turn right, but after ten minutes we realise she is wrong. We don't recognise anything.

'Oh my God, we are going to be so late getting back and they'll be furious,' she whimpers.

'Let's just find our way to the station and worry about what they'll say to us later,' I tell her.

Half an hour later, we're still lost in the labyrinth of side streets.

'I think we're in the red light district,' whispers Anna,

clinging to me tightly as we turn onto Brooke Street. I zip my red jumper right up to my chin and button up my coat.

'Oh my God, look at that!' I whisper back to her as we pass a shop with some very dubious and painful looking things in the window, the likes of which I have never seen before. We pass a doorway with a busty lady hovering in the shadows and a red light shining from the window above.

'Just don't look,' I say to Anna, who is on the verge of tears now.

Suddenly, out of nowhere, a man jumps in front of us and Anna screams. The man follows us for a while muttering something, but he soon gives up when he gets no more reaction from us. It's really scary, but we carry on walking and staring straight ahead. I'm amazed how calm I am, but I think it's because if I let myself get too scared we will really be in trouble, so I keep myself in control and we cling to each other even more tightly.

'We'll be fine,' I tell Anna. 'We'll find a respectable-looking woman and ask her the way to the station. Just calm down.'

We turn a corner and all of a sudden everything looks completely different. We are in a festive, brightly lit street with lanterns and Chinese dragons hanging everywhere and lots of people walking lazily around as if they are on a Sunday stroll. We see restaurants with strange-looking food displayed in the windows, and tables packed with families out for a meal.

'This must be Chinatown,' says Anna with a sigh of relief. 'Stavros told me about it. Thank God we are out of that terrible area.'

'Now we can ask the way to the Underground,' I say and start breathing normally again.

Once we are sitting safely on the train on our way back to Edgware, we relax enough to start worrying about what our parents are going to say when we get home. It's half past five, so we are already half an hour late. The journey seems to take forever. The train is slower than a turtle. Our fabulous day is turning into a disaster.

'We can't tell them we got talking to two boys and lost track of time,' says Anna, biting her nails with worry.

'But we *can* tell them we got lost, can't we?'

'I suppose so, but they're not going to think much of us, and they probably won't let us do it again if they think we are so useless.'

'Well, we've got to tell them something, so we better come up with a story – otherwise, bye-bye freedom.'

'OK, how about if we say we just got carried away in the shops and didn't realise the time, and then got caught up in the rush hour?'

'Worth a try,' I say, 'and in a way, it's not even lying, because strictly speaking we did get carried away and lost track of time, and we got caught up in something . . .' A smile starts up on my face for the first time since we left the coffee bar, which turns into a giggle and ends in great bursts of laughter from both of us.

Two stone-faced fathers, half frozen to death, are waiting for us at the station.

'You are an hour and a half late. We nearly called the police!' my father says sternly.

'You have a lot of explaining to do,' *Kyrios* Petros adds in the car on the way home.

Our story is accepted by both sets of parents, but we still get a lecture about responsibility and keeping our word and taking others into account and the dangers that lurk everywhere in a big city like London. We both promise we will be more careful and more thoughtful next time.

We are in the middle of showing our mothers our day's shopping when Tony and Stavros walk into the living room on their way out to the cinema.

'So, you finally found your way home?' says Stavros. 'What happened, then? Got lost in the big bad city, did you?'

'Not at all!' we both protest, perhaps a bit too much.

'I told you there would be trouble,' Tony says to our mothers as he walks out of the room.

CHAPTER SEVEN

A New Friend

Apart from giving us a fright, our adventure in the West End of London also gave us confidence, and made me realise that I am a lot tougher than I, or anyone else, had suspected. Even though we are pleased that we were able to cope with a crisis, neither of us want to repeat the experience again in a hurry, so we decide to keep our shopping expeditions close to home for a while.

I'm dying to tell some of the girls in my class about what happened, because I know I would go up in their estimation, but I also know it is too complicated a thing for me to explain. I just don't have the vocabulary.

Some of the girls at school are starting to be nice to me, now that they've got over the initial shock of having an alien amongst them. Linda is the first one to give me a sign that she likes me. We are standing in the dinner queue waiting for our food when she starts talking to me. I'm beginning to understand quite a lot of what the girls are saying around me now, but I am still finding it really hard to express myself. I never initiate a conversation – instead I always wait to be asked something and then try to answer.

Holding a plate of food containing some kind of unidentifiable meat and over-cooked vegetables, which always give me indigestion for the rest of the day, I make my way to a table and Linda comes and sits next to me. She is a tall, dark girl, with small but very dark brown eyes and black shiny, wavy hair. If I didn't know she was English I might think that she was Greek. But there are definitely no Greeks at this school.

'How do you like it here?' she asks me, speaking slowly and taking care to pronounce each word carefully.

'It is nice,' I reply and lower my eyes, hoping she doesn't go on to ask me something I can't answer. More than anything, it is the feeling of frustration that gets to me. I know what I want to say, but it just keeps coming out wrong. 'Why' and 'where' are the words I mix up the most.

'What about the cold?' she asks.

'It is very cold, I don't like, but I like the snow,' I say and beam with pleasure at having put together a whole sentence.

'What language do you speak in your country?' she asks.

'Greek.'

'Are you from Greece, then?'

'No, I am from Cyprus. I am Greek Cypriot.'

'Where do you live?'

'Edgware,' I say, and then try to ask her a question back. 'Why do you live?' I ask her and then seeing her puzzled expression, immediately realise that I made my usual mistake.

'Oh no, no!' I say. '*Where* do you live?'

She seems to understand my mistake and smiles at me, then we both burst out laughing. She is so nice and doesn't seem to mind that I don't understand everything.

'I live in Colindale,' she tells me. 'Do you want to come to my house one day after school?' she asks, smiling.

'Yes!' I say, smiling back.

I made a new friend at school,' I tell my mum over dinner.

'Is she Greek?' she asks.

'No. I told you I'm the only Greek girl at this school. She's English, but she's so nice. She really tries to be my friend, even though we can't talk to each other much. She's invited me to her house one day!'

I tell Anna about Linda too while we are watching TV after dinner. Anna already has some friends from school and she's pleased for me. 'That's great,' she says. 'She can come out with us sometimes, if you like her enough.'

I'm standing in a queue with Linda, waiting to buy a drink at break-time. There is a bunch of girls who have a tendency to push and bully people and boast about boys and wear a lot of make-up in school. In front of us is a girl called Susie, who thinks a lot of herself and is considered the gang leader by the others. She reminds me of the 'big girls' at the other school who wanted to shag my brother, and I keep my distance from her. Suddenly I'm aware that Susie's eyes have locked onto me and she is speaking to me. I freeze. Her body language is aggressive and so is her voice, and although I understand her words, what she's saying doesn't immediately make sense to me.

'What toothpaste do you use?' I think I hear her say, as if she is telling me to get out of her face. I'm paralyzed and I look to Linda for help. Linda repeats Susie's words to me slowly in case I didn't understand. It's simple, it's only a few easy words and I know what 'toothpaste' means.

When I establish that she is actually asking me something about *using* toothpaste, I assume that she must be mocking me and that she thinks I don't use it or have bad breath or something. Eventually, in the same aggressive manner, Susie tells Linda that the reason she's asking is that she thinks my teeth are pearly white and wants to get the same toothpaste as me. How incredible! She was complimenting me not insulting me! I still have a lot to learn.

'Do you want to come to my house for tea?' Linda asks after Susie has left us to join her mates. 'Come on a Sunday and then we can spend longer together,' she says, smiling.

'Your dad will take you there in the car,' Mum tells me while she's preparing dinner, 'so he can meet her parents.'

'Oh, Mama, I'm not a baby. It's embarrassing!' I protest.

'They're English, we don't know them, and you've never been to their house before,' she says firmly. 'I'm sure it'll be fine and you'll get to see how English people live – and find out what they offer people for tea,' she adds in a lighter tone.

What you offer people to eat when they come to your house for a visit is very important in our country and essential to the art of hospitality. 'Hospitality' is a sacred word for the Greeks, a matter of honour and national pride. Whole nations and cultures are judged by their hospitality, or their lack of it, and unfortunately the English don't rate very high in this department in my mother's eyes.

'Remember when Maria and Andreas went to visit those English relations of Maria's?' she continues, rolling her eyes. 'They got nothing to eat for a whole day! How hospitable is that? You invite people to your home and just give them a cup of tea and send them on their way!'

My mother and every member of my family still have not recovered from my auntie Maria and uncle Andrea's ordeal of going on a visit and getting nothing to eat. They were invited for tea at her sister-in-law's and when they were asked if they would like some cake with their tea, they replied with the customary 'No, thank you', which in our culture is the polite thing to do. But unfortunately, the English in-laws took them at their word. In Cyprus, you never say 'yes' straight away, because it seems far too eager and impolite. But when you decline, you know that you will be asked again several times. In the meantime, while you are saying your 'No, thank you, don't go to any trouble', the hostess is busy laying out the cakes, biscuits, sandwiches, stuffed vine leaves, cheese pastries, and gallons of refreshments, in front of her guests. No one takes notice of these refusals and after the offer has been refused a third time, everyone tucks in.

'A lousy cup of tea,' my uncle said when they got back. 'We were there five hours and all we got was a cup of tea!

In my village we give people tea when they're sick, not when they go visiting.'

'You be sure that when you go to your friend's, you take whatever food is offered to you the first time you are asked,' Mum warns me as she dishes out our supper. 'I don't want you spending the whole day starving!'

CHAPTER EIGHT

It's in the Coffee Grounds

It's Saturday morning and we are sitting in Anna's kitchen while our mothers are making Greek coffee so they can read the coffee grounds. The sky is covered in one big, flat grey cloud, without a glimpse of sunshine peeking through. The light has an almost green tinge to it and although it's not actually raining the atmosphere outside is incredibly damp – perfect weather to frizz up your hair . . . Everyone's mood is low and it seems that it's been weeks since any of us have seen the sun.

The letter I got this morning from my cousin Sophia hasn't helped much either, as she describes sitting in the sunshine as she wrote to me. I wish I was sitting in the sun talking to Sophia with Chloe curled up on my lap and listening to music. I miss them both so much. I've been trying to convince Anna that perhaps we could get a kitten to share, but she won't have any of it. 'As if there aren't enough people crammed into this house,' she said to me. 'We definitely don't need a pet as well!' I suppose she is right. Even if she thought it was a good idea, our mothers definitely wouldn't, so I don't know why I even bothered . . . Still, the warm cosy kitchen is the best place to be this morning and the smell of the freshly brewed coffee is very comforting.

Suddenly the telephone rings and makes us all jump.

'Answer the phone, Anna,' her mum says. 'I can't leave the coffee; it will boil over, and anyway, it's probably for you.'

Anna and I are in the middle of looking at the fashion pages in a magazine, so she gets up rather grumpily to take the call. When she returns her face is flushed and she signals for me to follow her into the other room.

'Oh my god!' she hisses. 'It was that guy, Peter, the one we met in town at the coffee bar! Remember, I gave him my number? I've been dreading this.'

'Thank God *you* answered the phone,' I say. 'Can you imagine if Tony or Stavros had answered it?' We weren't too worried about our mothers, with the state of their English. 'What did he say?'

'Well, they want to take us out,' she says, flushing again, right down to her neck.

'Us . . . ? They? You mean his friend the art student – Tom?' I say and feel a flutter in my stomach.

'Well, yes, they obviously liked us and they want to go on a date or something . . . I don't know, I've never been on a date – and with an English boy too!' she says and she looks sick.

'Well, that's not so bad,' I say. 'They were nice, but how are we going to do that? When do they want to meet? What did *you* say?'

'I said I would think about it and call him back.'

'We can't go into town again. We'll have to ask them to come up here or something.'

'Oh God, I don't know,' says Anna. 'What are we going to say to everyone? We don't exactly go out clubbing on our own all the time, do we?'

'But we do go to the cinema, so they can come and see a film with us and then we can have a coffee with them after, can't we? That way we don't have to tell anyone anything or lie. We just meet them at the cinema.'

'I suppose so. Yes, it's a good idea,' says Anna and her spirits lift again.

'When do you need to call him back? When do they want to meet?' I ask.

'I didn't say, but it's up to us. I just said I would call him back soon.'

'Fine, let's meet them next weekend,' I say cheerfully. 'Saturday, because I'm going to Linda's house on Sunday. Now, let's go and get our coffee grounds read. The coffee must be ready by now!'

Our mothers are in the middle of reading each other's grounds when we come back into the kitchen.

'My turn next,' announces Anna, 'and then Ioulia's. We want to know everything!'

My mum pours equal amounts of coffee into our tiny cups and the thick, sweet liquid trickles down our throats easily. Mum thinks I'm too young to drink Greek coffee because it's too strong, but I like having my grounds read, so I've convinced myself I like it.

After we drink it, we turn the cups upside down on the saucers and wait till the grounds dry. The patterns made by the grounds are dense and dark and very intricate and many things can be interpreted by the shape they create on the white of the china cup. Anna's mum is the expert and as she puts her glasses on to look at her daughter's cup first, we sit in anticipation. Perfect timing – we might learn something about our forthcoming dates.

'Well, well,' says *Kyria* Eva, 'what is this I see? A tall visitor with blue eyes! Be careful of blue eyes, Anna, they bring bad luck. The evil eye! Who do you know with blue eyes?' she asks, then she suddenly realises that she made a mistake and she is reading my cup, not Anna's.

'It must be you, then, Ioulia. Do you know anyone with blue eyes?'

'Well, of course I do. We live in England – I know dozens of people with blue eyes now,' I tell her, blushing when I remember Tom, with his mesmerising blue eyes looking at me in the coffee bar!

'It could be anyone,' I say casually, picking up Anna's cup and handing it over.

'Let's see,' *Kyria* Eva says, peering into the cup, 'I see a crossroad, a decision that needs to be made . . . You are unsure, but I also see clear skies, which is a good thing.'

Anna and I look at each other, smiling, and we stop listening to all the other things she is telling us about seeing school books and exam papers.

Anna makes the phone call and we are all set to meet outside our local cinema next Saturday.

Let's hope Tony and Stavros don't decide to go and see a film next Saturday too . . .

CHAPTER NINE

Secret Date

We've been nervous all week in anticipation of our date with the English boys. We both know very well that our parents would disapprove. As if it's not enough that I'm considered far too young to be dating anyone, the boys are not even Greek!

'So-and-so's daughter has a *boyfriend,*' my mum mentions every so often. The mere word 'boyfriend' evokes thoughts of naughty girls misbehaving, doing all sorts of things they shouldn't. This comment is generally followed by something like, 'She's too advanced for her age, and they obviously don't exercise enough control over her. A *boyfriend,* at *her* age! When the time comes for a boyfriend, Ioulia *mou,* you will go out with a nice Greek boy, from a good family.'

But here we are, all dressed up and on our way to see a couple of English boys we met in a coffee bar in the West End, who our parents have never even seen! What could we be thinking? Our nervous excitement makes us feel almost sick.

'I hope they are as good-looking as we remember them,' says Anna, 'so this is worth all the stress.'

'If we don't like them, we don't have to see them again,' I say.

'Who says we are going to see them again? First of all, they might not ask us out again, and second, I don't know if I can cope with all the anxiety!'

The two boys are waiting for us just inside the lobby of the cinema, and both look far from disappointing. They obviously talked about which one of us each of them liked, because Tom insists on buying me my ticket and Peter buys Anna's.

It is all very new and strange. I am tingling with excitement but also fear. In the darkness of the theatre, we sit paired up like we are two couples. When Tom tries to put his arm around me, I freeze. Oh my God! Does he think he is my *boyfriend*? But the cinema, I realise, is the perfect place to meet for a date because we don't have to talk. He smiles at me, I smile back, and we just sit and watch the film, understanding as much as I can.

Outside, on the way to a café for a coffee, Tom takes my hand. I think it is such a sweet gesture, but feel terrified that someone might see us. It is an irrational fear, because we don't know anyone – the dreaded brothers are at a party and our parents are most definitely not out and about. But years of conditioning (nice girls don't do such things with boys they don't know) makes me feel anxious, even though I can't see what's so wrong.

At the café, Anna translates and Tom keeps smiling and looking at me with his piercing blue eyes. I decide there and then I have to learn English as soon as possible, because apart from everything else, I wanted to be able to talk to him.

'Well, I'm definitely going to see him again,' I tell Anna as soon as we leave them to make our way home.

'Me too,' she says, 'but I told them not to phone at the house again. I said we'd call them.'

I'm dying to tell someone else about Tom. It occurs to me to tell Linda, since I'm spending the afternoon with her at her house tomorrow, but it would be hard. I feel sure that she would be a really good person to tell my secrets to, but I will have to wait a little longer, till I know more words. The person I really need to talk to about this is Sophia, but I'm reluctant to write to her in case her mum reads it and tells my mum. Reading other people's letters is yet another one of those activities Greek parents think there is nothing wrong with – a bit like the 'privacy' thing – so I don't want to risk it. I call Stella instead, because I know she will love the gossip and it's just the sort of thing she wants to hear. These days we talk to each other a couple of times a week, and meet up sometimes at the weekends.

'You lucky thing!' she screams down the phone. 'I can't believe it! You're only there five minutes and you get a boyfriend!'

'He's not my boyfriend – he's just a boy I like,' I protest. 'I fancy him because he's really gorgeous and artistic, but I'm not going to start going out with him all the time or anything. It's too stressful, as Anna says. And besides, he is eighteen, which I suppose is younger than I thought, but if he knew how old I was, he'd run a mile!'

'When are you seeing him again?'

'I don't know. We'll call and make an arrangement in a couple of weeks, but I don't want to say anything to my parents. They'll go mad.'

'I've convinced my parents to let me have a party for my birthday in three weeks, so why don't you bring him to that? You can come with Anna and the other guy too!' she says excitedly.

'What a brilliant idea,' says Anna when I tell her. 'We can always rely on Stella to come up with something good! That would be great! We'll meet them there – no one needs to know.'

'Honestly, Papa, how old do you think I am? You didn't drop me off when I went to visit my friends in Cyprus. It's so embarrassing! What are you going to say to her parents?' I moan to my dad as he drives me to Linda's house the next day.

'I just want to say hello so they know we are nice people and I can see what kind of people they are,' he says.

'What kind of people do you think they are going to be? They are normal people like us.'

'I know, but it's your first visit to someone's house here and I want to be sure everything is OK,' he insists. If only he knew who Anna and I had been seeing without his 'OK' . . . I try to put the thought out of my mind.

Linda lives in a big, detached house with front and back gardens (very English), bay windows and a garage. I find English houses boring. Everything is designed for staying indoors. I miss verandas and balconies – I just want to be outside all the time, but usually it's freezing.

Linda's dad is out, so it's her mother who opens the door and invites my dad into the living room for some coffee. She returns with a freshly brewed pot of aromatic coffee and a plate full of home-baked biscuits. I can see by my dad's expression as he accepts the offerings that he's pleased. Linda and I sit with the two of them for a while as they chat. Linda's mum is a very attractive, dark-haired, woman with dark eyes – and she's very warm and friendly. She asks my dad lots of questions about Cyprus and his work. I can see he is impressed.

'What a lovely gentleman your father is,' she says to me after he leaves. 'It must be very hard for all of you coming here from such a lovely warm country.'

'My great-grandparents came from Russia,' Linda tells me slowly, pronouncing each word carefully, while we listen to music in her bedroom. 'They had to leave everything behind because they were Jewish, and then my grandparents had to run away from the Nazis in Germany to save their lives.'

'Oh,' I say, 'I thought you are English.'

'We are English,' she replies. 'It's just that we are Jewish.'

I'm not quite sure what that means. We learned about the persecution of the Jews at school in Cyprus, but I thought that was in Germany. I didn't realise you could be English *and* Jewish. I make a mental note to ask Dad about it when I get home.

'By the way,' says Linda, 'it's my brother's bar mitzvah next Saturday and I would like you to come – would you like to?'

'What is bar mitzvah?' I ask.

Linda tries to explain, but I'm lost and I don't understand, so I make another mental note to ask my dad.

'It's a big party,' she finally says. 'It's good fun! You'll come, yes?'

'Yes,' I say. 'I love parties!'

Linda's mum calls us to go downstairs for tea. The dining room table is laid out with as many cakes as my auntie Eleni would have laid out if she was having guests. It is packed with gorgeous food – cakes, biscuits and sandwiches, and a huge pot of tea in the middle. I gaze at all of it in amazement, and for a moment I think I must be in a Cypriot household, until I hear Linda's mum telling us to sit down.

'Well, how was it?' Mum asks as soon as Dad and I walk into the house.

'Just like us,' I tell her. 'Her mother made as many cakes and food as you do, and she kept telling me to have more, just like you do.'

'Was it tasty?'

'Lovely – only they didn't have any spanakopita or dolmades, but everything else was nearly the same!'

'Was it English food?' she asks. 'Are they English?'

'Yes,' I say, 'they are, but they're Jewish too. Papa, what is Jewish?'

CHAPTER TEN

A Glimpse of Another Culture

'Jewish is a faith,' my dad explains. 'They believe in the Old Testament and they are still waiting for the son of God to come. Basically, they don't believe in Jesus.'

'So are there Jewish people all over the world?'

'Yes, and that's partly because all through history they were persecuted, so they tried to make their homes in places where it was safe. Many of them now live in Israel.'

'Isn't Cyprus safe for them? I never met a Jewish person there.'

'I don't know. I suppose there must be some Jewish people there . . .' Dad says, trying to remember.

'Is their religion the only thing that's different from other English people?'

'I really don't know,' Dad says thoughtfully. 'All I do know is that your friend's mother was very different to most of the English people I've ever met. But then I don't know that many.'

The work my dad does in London is with a Greek shipping company and, although there are a few English people working there, the majority of his colleagues are

Greek, so meeting someone like Linda's mum was as much of a surprise for Dad as it was for me. His previous knowledge of English people was based on the British colonists that governed our country before independence, when my dad was a young man and Cyprus was under British rule. They had very upper-class accents and what he described as superiority complexes. The first time he saw an English person that was not like that was at Victoria Station the day we arrived in England. Up until then, my dad had only ever met the tall, fair-haired, pale-skinned type and he stared in disbelief at the short, dark man who was pushing a trolley piled high with luggage and being ordered around by a big fat lady in a hat.

'A porter!' he said, turning around to look at Mum, Tony and me. 'An *English* porter,' he whispered in astonishment. Then, with great pleasure, he beckoned the porter over and, in his heavily accented English, he instructed him to load *our* luggage on his trolley, even though it was only a few feet to the car of the distant relative who was picking us up.

'Linda has invited me to go to her brother's bar mitzvah party next Saturday. What is bar mitzvah? And can I go?' I ask Dad.

'I believe it's a ceremony to celebrate the coming of age of teenage boys.'

'I know what it is,' my mum joins in, while she's chopping vegetables. 'It's like the Turks. The Muslims have something similar – I think they call it circumcision. Don't you remember, Yianni?' she says, looking at my dad.

'We went to one, years ago, in that village. They had a celebration for the son of that Turkish colleague of yours . . .' My mother tends to remember every single, minute detail about things, people and occasions and she goes on about them at length. She knows quite a lot about Turkish customs as the two communities were very integrated when she was growing up and she had lots of Turkish friends. Her best friend was Hatice *Hanum*, a lovely Turkish neighbour, with whom she spent most of her days before the troubles started and the two communities were separated. She never forgot Hatice and all the fun they used to have together. Hatice has a son in London and he's promised that he will bring his mother over at some point for a visit so the two friends can be reunited.

'Yes, I think I do, but I really don't think it's a circumcision at the age of thirteen,' Dad says, looking horrified. 'I'm sure it's just a ceremony and a party. And of course it's fine for you to go, Ioulia.'

'What's for dinner – and what are you all talking about?' Tony asks, poking his head round the kitchen door.

'Mousaka,' Mum tells him cheerfully. 'Are you hungry? It will be ready soon, and Ioulia's been telling us that she's been invited to a circumcision party!'

'What to wear to your brother's party?' I ask Linda as we walk around the playground at break-time.

'A party dress.'

'I give him present?'

'Yes, if you like,' she answers, smiling, and I make a

54

mental note to ask my mother what to buy a thirteen-year-old boy.

The lights are very bright in the ballroom and the music the band is playing seems strangely familiar to me. Dozens of tables are decorated with beautiful flowers, glasses and plates, and the guests are all dressed up in their finery. It feels like a wedding, I think as I watch the waiters serving food. Linda's brother, Joshua, is being kissed and hugged and showered with presents and her parents seem to be radiating with happiness and pride. I sit at one of the tables with Linda and some of her cousins, feeling dazzled by the spectacle before me. Wow! Linda's family must be *so* rich, I think to myself. Food, wine and champagne flow freely and everyone is talking and laughing – but I understand nothing apart from what Linda tells me. She really knows how to talk to me to make me understand. I tell her and she says it's because her great-grandmother from Russia could barely speak English, so she had to speak slowly and carefully to her like she does with me.

'Lucky Joshua. He's got so many presents,' she says. 'Some girls have this celebration, but I didn't want one.' She giggles. 'I'll just wait till I get married and have an even bigger party and *more* presents.'

The band plays a tune that I have heard a thousand times in Cyprus, and for some reason I know all the words – although I don't know what language it is – so I start singing with everyone else. People are clapping along to the tune and dancing.

'How do you know this song?' asks Linda, puzzled. 'This is like a Jewish anthem. It's called "Hava Nagila" – it's in Hebrew!'

'I don't know . . . I hear it on radio in my country, and it's well known,' I tell her. 'It's from Israel, I think.'

'*I* don't even know all the words,' she says.

'What do the words mean?' I ask her.

'I have no idea.'

'But everyone is singing them,' I say, astonished.

'So are you, and *you* don't know what it means,' she replies. 'I've just grown up with it, but I don't speak the language.'

We clap along to the tune and Linda pulls me from my chair and we join the dancing. I can't believe it – it's like being back home! The dancing, the music, all the friendly people. It's so familiar and comforting. For the first time since arriving in England I feel at home outside my own house.

CHAPTER ELEVEN

Into Deep Water

'There's a letter for you from Cyprus,' shouts Tony from downstairs on his way out. 'It's probably from one of your heartbroken boyfriends,' he says mockingly, and I nearly break my neck running down the stairs to pick it up. I wait longingly every month for this letter. I know it's from my cousin Sophia because she is the only one I write to. Letter-writing is such a pain, even though I love getting them. I tear the envelope open and wallow in the sheer pleasure of the vision of blue ink on the airmail tissue paper she always writes on.

'*HELP! I'm drowning here!*' she writes. '*I can't breathe, it's so boring, and you are so far away!*'

My uncle is very strict and keeps my cousins on a tight rein, and so they all rebel. When I was there, she had me to moan to and do things with, but now she is stuck with her older sisters, who like Tony, take no notice of her.

I take my letter off to the bedroom and close the door behind me. I sit cross-legged on the bed in a pool of early spring sunshine coming through the window, and give myself up to the joy of reading all the news from home.

'Maria started going out with Luca, and Anastasia is heartbroken,' she writes. Luca is the school heart-throb, and last year everyone was after him – and from what I read, everyone still is. 'Everyone keeps asking how you are, and I saw Marco the other day, and he started complaining that you never write to him.' Marco is a boy who used to fancy me, but I can't see the point in keeping in touch with him. I never liked him that much . . . 'I went to Bapu's house on Sunday and saw Chloe,' she carries on. ('Bapu' is the word for 'grandfather' in Greek.) 'She's fine, but I think she really misses you, because she wouldn't leave me alone the whole time I was there. She spent the entire visit sitting on my lap.'

The mention of Chloe makes me feel really sad. I so wished I had her sitting curled up beside me on the bed right now.

'Bapu said that next time you write to him to also enclose a photo of yourself in your school uniform outside the house.' I love my grandfather and miss him very much. Although he is very old, he is really fit and healthy. Since my grandmother died four years ago he's lived on his own, but he keeps very busy and sociable and of course he's never left alone for very long . . .

At the end of Sophia's letter there is some great news. My aunt and uncle have decided they will come and visit us in London in the summer! So at last Sophia and I will be together again even if it's only for a few weeks. I jump off the bed and rush to tell my mum.

'I know,' she says. 'I meant to tell you. We talked on the phone last week and we decided we would all take a trip together to Spain for a week while they are here.'

A double treat! I'm beside myself with excitement, because apart from Greece and the countries we darted through by train on our way to England, I have never been *anywhere*. Our journey to London seems like a dream now. The ship we boarded on the Cypriot shores, then the train through Europe and the traumatic channel crossing from France, when the whole family was sea-sick to the point of collapse, was becoming a distant memory. However, the shrinking figures of our relatives who came to see us sail off on the *Apollonian*, and the ever-growing space between me and Cyprus still lingers in my mind. I can see my auntie waving us off with her big white handkerchief, and the dark, sombre figure of my grandfather standing silent and still on the shore.

But I know *this* will be a completely different journey and the excitement makes me tingle.

'We are going to Spain in the summer with my cousins,' I tell Anna.

'I told you by the summer things would be better. In a few months you'll be speaking much more English too!'

'They speak Spanish in Spain, so English is not going to help me much . . . but I think I'll leave learning Spanish for another year,' I say and we both laugh.

'Now, how about this party at Stella's,' says Anna. 'What are we going to say to the boys? Is Stella's mum going to be there? Because if she is, forget it.'

'No, Stella said her parents were going out. Her big brother will stay and keep an eye on things. He's OK – not like our two.'

'So let's make the phone call and give them the address!'

We spend the whole afternoon getting ready for the party and we both agree we look great.

'I'm so nervous,' Anna says as we are putting the finishing touches to our make-up. 'I hope we are doing the right thing. I'm not exactly sure what they expect. I really like Peter and he seems so intelligent, but I can't spend all night just talking to him. It's a party!'

'At least you *can* talk to him. All I do is smile and nod. And you won't be there to translate either, so I dread to think what's going to happen with me,' I say, suddenly feeling very sick.

'Your English is so much better now, Ioulia,' Anna says encouragingly, 'and you understand so much more. You'll be fine with him. Just ask him to speak slowly.' She shrugs her shoulders. 'Anyway, we'll have to see how it goes – too late now to have second thoughts.'

Stella's house is about half an hour's drive away, and *Kyrios* Petros is taking us there.

'Now you make sure you call in good time when the party is over so I can come and collect you – and make sure it's not later than midnight,' he says, fussing as we both roll our eyes in the back of the car.

Stella opens the door to us and loud music and laughter spill out of the house, which is packed with people.

'I didn't know you knew so many people,' I shout over the noise as I walk in, bumping into furniture because it's so dark.

60

'My brother invited some of his friends too,' she says and apologises for the darkness as she takes our coats.

'My mum made me keep all the lights on, but I switched them off as soon as they left. Then I didn't have time to organise anything else. Luckily Theo is fine about it. He agrees that you can't have a party with all the lights on.'

Stella's brother, Theo, is nineteen and his girlfriend is there too. It's Stella's fifteenth birthday, so it's a big deal for her and she's decorated the room with balloons, streamers, some candles and a couple of lava lamps. It looks nice, but there's not exactly enough light to see what's going on.

'Shame Tony couldn't come,' she says. 'I might have convinced him that I'm old enough for him now.'

'Not a shame at all!' I snap back. 'We wouldn't have been able to invite Tom and Peter if he had.'

'Talking of which, where are they?' Stella asks, looking around.

'We asked them to meet us here,' says Anna. 'Can I have a drink now please – I'm really nervous.'

'There is beer, cider or Coke,' says Stella.

'What's cider?' I ask.

'Try it and see,' she says, smiling. 'It's great!'

'It's quite easy to drink,' warns Anna, 'so take it easy – you don't want to get drunk!'

I take note and sip the sweet, fizzy drink with caution. The last thing I want is to get drunk at the first party I go to in London, with a strange boy I hardly know.

We both jump when the doorbell rings. Stella calls for

us as Tom and Peter walk into the hall with a bunch of other guests. As expected, they both look very good, and Stella looks on approvingly, winking at us behind their backs. Tom gives me a kiss on the cheek, and I blush not knowing what to say. There is nothing I *can* say, so I get them both a drink, and realise that the only thing I'll be able to do with Tom this evening is dance.

We must have been dancing non-stop for two hours by the time Tom gently puts his arms around my waist and tries to kiss me on the lips. I'm overwhelmed with shyness and look away. I feel as if I'm going red from my head to my toes, and that the heat which is radiating from my body can be felt by everyone. I've had the odd little fleeting kiss with boys at parties in Cyprus, but they were boys my age who knew even less than I did about kissing. This feels different. Tom looks serious and intense and I don't really know how to respond to him. Suddenly he takes my hand and leads me out of the living room towards the room where all our coats are. It's dark and quiet in there, with only the gentle thumping of the bass line coming from the other room. Maybe he wants to try and talk to me quietly, I think to myself, as we take a seat on the bed.

He slowly pulls me towards him. He kisses me gently on the lips and I like it. I can see his blue eyes glistening in the dark. He smells faintly of aftershave and his lips are soft and warm. Shyly, I kiss him back and my heart starts to thump. He talks to me gently and a few words break through the haze that's in my head, but I don't really understand what he's saying.

I drift along with his kisses and suddenly I find myself lying on the bed, sinking gently into the warm folds of all the coats. I feel Tom's hand gently caressing my leg and then I feel his hand on my thigh and moving up under my skirt. I'm wearing lots of clothes, with thick, woolly tights as well, but the realisation of what he is doing makes me bolt upright. I think my heart is going to burst through my chest and I'm sure he can hear it thumping. I can't believe what I'm doing. What am I thinking of? I'm on a bed, getting off with a boy four years older than me, who thinks I'm at least two years older than I am, and I've only ever met him three times . . . and I don't even understand anything he says to me!

'No!' I say to him and jump from the bed.

'OK,' he says, smiling. Then he takes my hand and leads me back into the other room.

On the way home, I sit silently in the back of the car while Anna's dad gives us the third degree on how our evening went. I had no chance to say anything to her and I badly need to talk through everything with my friend. But I know that when we get home the rest of the family will still be awake and there will be no chance for us to be on our own.

I lay awake in bed, thinking, long after Tony starts snoring. I come to the decision that Tom is too grown-up for me. I'm nowhere near ready to have the kind of relationship he seems to be looking for. I'm also confused about how I feel. I keep playing back in my head the scene on the bed and I realise that apart from being excited and enjoying the kissing and touching, what I felt most of all was fear. It was unknown territory, an experience I've never had before and these new feelings are troubling me. Not being able to talk to Tom is a problem too. It makes me feel powerless. Perhaps that's it, I decide. I should wait until I understand a little more of what boys are saying to me before I get involved with them in that way. But then again, I really like Tom, so perhaps I should wait and see . . .

CHAPTER TWELVE

Getting Into a Muddle

My father has decided that I need extra tuition in English, so he has asked Miss Hammond if she would teach me on Saturday mornings. I'm not keen at first, because that's the day I sleep late and then go out and spend time with Anna.

'It's the only way you'll make fast progress,' he tells me, and I know he's right. 'You spend too much time talking in Greek with Anna anyway. Once your English starts to improve, it won't matter so much.'

Miss Hammond lives in a very nice leafy area of London and she answers the door to us in her bare feet, which my dad thinks is scandalous.

'She had no shoes on!' he tells Mum later. 'I don't understand how she could open the door to people half-dressed!'

Personally, I think it's fine. I read in a magazine that if you can, you should leave your feet bare, because it's good for them, so obviously she's read the same article in the English *Cosmopolitan* or something.

I don't see any evidence of anyone else living with Miss

Hammond, like a boyfriend or husband or children. We sit in a glass room full of plants and for an hour she does reading and writing with me. There are three cats who sit with us during the lesson, purring in the sunshine. One of them, with dark chocolate-coloured fur and yellow eyes, reminds me of Chloe and likes to jump on my lap. As I feel her warm fur and loud purring, my mind wanders off to another sunny room, two thousand miles away in our house in Nicosia, where my mum would sit and sew and I would sit by her, playing with my cat.

'I think it's best if we take Chloe to your grandfather's house soon,' my mum tells me. 'Best to do it well before we leave so that she gets use to it.' I stroke Chloe's warm fur and hug her close. I can't bear to let her go; but my mother insists it's for the best.

We take her by car to my grandfather's, which is several miles away from our house, right through the city into the old part of town. I am heartbroken, but there is nothing I can do, and I feel guilty for abandoning her.

Then, one morning about two weeks later, Mum comes into my room and wakes me up and then leads me into the hall, where an exhausted Chloe is lying on the cool tiles, panting and waiting for me. She looks bedraggled, her fur is matted and there's a tired look in her eyes, having braved the city traffic and walked right through the streets of the capital to find her way back to our house. The minute she sees me, she summons up all her strength and jumps into my arms. I can't believe it, even though I've heard of animals doing this before. I always thought they were just sentimental stories.

'She really is your faithful cat,' my mum says as I wipe the

tears from my eyes. 'Once we're gone, she'll sense it and she'll settle in at your grandfather's house,' she carries on, trying to comfort me.

'Are you OK, Julia?' asks Miss Hammond, bringing me back to the present with a start, as I'm still stroking her cat.

'Yes,' I say and I would really like to tell her about Chloe, but I don't feel I have enough words yet, so I make a promise to myself to practise so I can try and tell her soon.

Monday is PE day at school and I dread it more than any other day. I've been at this new school for nearly three months now, and I've had three months worth of hellish Mondays! Even though I seem to be good at sport and really enjoy running, I dread the end of Games when we all have to change in a communal changing room. Undressing, as far as I'm concerned, is a private matter – even though the Greeks are not big on privacy, when it comes to taking your clothes off, privacy *does* apply. I find undressing in front of twenty other girls, some of whom don't look like they have even hit puberty yet, very unpleasant. I make excuses whenever I can to avoid Mondays by pretending I'm ill so I can have a day off, or take a note in from my parents saying I've got a cold and can't participate. It doesn't work that often, so I sometimes have to suffer the humiliation.

I watch the other girls strip naked to change into their clean clothes, joking and laughing, and I feel like I want to die. Their lily-white bodies that almost seem to be tinged with blue, are still angular and shapeless and such a contrast to my dark skin and feminine curves. It's not enough that I have a full set of pubic hair, but I also have hairy legs, hairy arms, bushy eyebrows masses of curly hair that takes three days to dry (or seems to, anyway), and in comparison to them, I also have a moustache! Stripped naked, I feel like a chimp. I realise that I can't go on for the next two years not doing PE and avoiding the shower thing, but right now I don't know how to deal with it. I don't really want to talk to Linda, who doesn't seem to mind too much, about it either, because it highlights the difference between me and everybody else.

'It's so humiliating,' I told Anna last night. 'The other girls – apart from a few – look so young and some of them don't even wear a bra yet.'

'You know,' Anna said, 'next year you probably won't have to do it anymore – like in my school, I think they make it optional after a certain age. Wait and see.'

Next year seems a lifetime away, and anyway, the other girls will probably have caught up with me by then – although I doubt if any of them will sprout as much body hair as me.

It's the spring term, and the snow has melted. We're doing PE outside in the fields much more and I find myself running and competing a lot. In my school in Cyprus I was always good at sport and a good runner, and I'm pleased to discover that I have been selected to be in a running team, although I'm not sure I understand what the team is training for. My PE teacher is very encouraging and keeps saying, 'Good, good' and 'Well done' to me. We are training very vigorously for something, which I think must be Sports Day. Linda has explained to me that it's a day we do sports in a field and all the school comes to watch us.

The morning of the Sports Day, there is a lot of commotion in the school and I'm being fussed over by my PE teacher, who keeps saying things I don't understand and I keep nodding. If only I could understand what other people are telling me as well as I understand Linda and Miss Hammond, things would be a lot easier.

We all arrive at the sports field, which is packed with not only girls but what look like parents too. I'm ushered onto a track with a whole lot of other girls I have never seen – from another school, I think – and it seems they're expecting me to run with them.

Suddenly, looking at their uniforms, I click! I'm representing my school in a running race against three other schools, and the race is about to start! Oh my God! I freeze and break into a sweat. Why didn't I realise that's what all the training was about? It was all such a muddle. My mouth is suddenly very dry. I look around the field and then at the terraces, with all the people, sitting and waiting for Sports Day to kick off with the first race. There is nothing I can do but go along with everything. As if in a dream, I take my place, feeling like I'm having an out-of-body experience. I can't believe it's me standing here and I keep thinking I'm imagining it all. Everything seems so unreal . . . I look at all the people and they seem to talk and move in slow motion and everything is slightly out of synch. I'm sure I will wake up in a minute. Suddenly I hear the whistle, and instantaneously everything reverts into sharp focus again and I run for my life to the end of the line, oblivious to anyone else around me. Panting and trying to catch my breath, I'm immediately surrounded by teachers and girls, cheering, grinning, and patting me on the back.

Miraculously, I have won the race, and the approval of my teachers and the other girls.

CHAPTER THIRTEEN

Planning a Feast

'I won a running race for my school today,' I tell everyone excitedly when I get home that day. 'And I got a medal!'

'What kind of race?' my mum asks in amazement.

'A running one,' I say, 'but I didn't even know I was doing it, otherwise you could have all come along to watch.'

'When did you find out?' asks Anna.

I tell them the whole story, and they all laugh, even more than the day my mum stood on a chair to change a light bulb and went right through it!

'It's time you took notice of what is being said to you,' Tony says patronisingly. 'You can get into trouble like that.'

'I *do* take notice!' I protest. 'It's just that what people say doesn't make any sense to me and I can't just keep saying "pardon?" all the time.'

I realise then that what is wrong with my life at the moment, is exactly that. Things aren't making sense. Just as I think I understand something, I find out I got it all wrong – from getting out of my depth with Tom, to the

Sports Day muddle. I'm almost there – I no longer feel deaf and dumb, like I did when I first arrived in England. My hearing is only partially impaired now and I'm learning to speak. The words are there and I *feel* I can run with them, that I can open my mouth and speak out. But when I actually try to speak, it's as if a piece of sellotape has been plastered over my mouth and I can't open it. The language is no longer a stream of incomprehensible babble, with no beginning or an end to it. I am starting to hear individual words and understand them. But once they are strung together in a slightly more complex sentence and delivered by someone other than Linda or Mrs Hammond, I'm lost in a grey cloud of isolation again. When will this cloud lift? And when will I start feeling as if I'm part of things?

The Easter holidays are almost here and the atmosphere is very festive at the school. There is a familiar feeling of end-of-term euphoria, just like I remember it in Cyprus. It's spring, which helps to lift everyones spirits – the long winter darkness is giving way to daylight at last, and it is turning milder. I'm delighted to see on my way to school that tulips are bursting through the soil and that fine green leaves and blossoms are starting to appear on the trees. Although Greeks usually celebrate Easter at a different time from the English, this year it has fallen at the same time.

Easter is our largest religious festival, and we are starting preparations for our first Easter away from home. Easter Sunday is the most fun. In Greece and Cyprus, people spill out into the open air to celebrate both the resurrection of Christ, and the signalling of spring. It's an eating, drinking, singing and dancing festival and usually celebrations take place in fields or by the sea or in people's gardens. No one stays inside and traditionally, families build huge fires and roast a whole pig, suckling lamb or baby goat on a spit, and spend all day and well into the evening, celebrating.

'If it's a nice day, we will roast the lamb in the garden,' says *Kyria* Eva.

'We can build a fire pit with bricks for the spit,' says Stavros.

'Are we cooking a whole animal?' asks Tony.

'Depends how many of us will be coming,' Mum replies.

'I'm sure that between us, we will invite a few,' *Kyria* Eva says. 'Who do you want to invite?' she asks, looking at my mum.

'Well, to start with, I suppose we should ask the two Greek men from Yianni's office. They don't have anyone here and Tony has a couple of friends at the college who are Greek and they don't have any family here either . . .'

'Can I invite Linda?' I interrupt my mum excitedly. 'Since I went to her brother's bar mitzvah?'

'Of course you can, but they might be doing their own celebrations.'

'I don't think they will. They are Jewish, remember – they don't believe in Jesus.'

'Why don't you see if your friend Stella and her family want to come? Do they have much family in England?'

'I don't know, but that would be great and you can meet her parents,' I tell her. 'You might all get on really well.'

The truth is, it's us who don't have family and friends here, and I can tell that our mothers are desperately trying to think of as many people as possible to expand their circle and to make our Easter as festive as it would be back home.

The two mothers make a list of about twenty-five people, including all of us, for the celebrations. It's a mix of Greeks from Cyprus and Greece who are living in London for one reason or another. There will be some student friends of Tony and Stavros, two of my dad's colleagues, a distant cousin of Anna's dad's who has lived in England for ten years, is married to a Spanish lady and works as a singer in a Greek club, and Stella's family. We're all very excited about the distant cousin, because we'll ask him to bring his guitar along. That's another thing about the Greeks – they never pass up an opportunity to sing and dance.

Tony has a Greek professor who has no family here, so Mum insists he is invited too. 'I don't know if I want my teacher here,' Tony protests.

'That's not very generous of you,' she says. 'Poor man on his own at Easter – it's unthinkable!'

My mother really makes me laugh! As much as she is hospitable and generous and charitable, it's obvious she is trying to enlarge her Greek social circle . . . But how can I blame her?

'Don't you want to invite anyone from your school?' I ask Anna.

'Not really, I'd like to invite Peter, but can you imagine the drama?' she says with a sigh.

Anna is really keen on Peter and was not happy when I told her I was going to cool it off with Tom.

'Does that mean you don't want to see him again?' she asked me, looking worried. I'd just finished telling her all about what happened on the bed.

'Well, I don't know . . . I just want to take it easy for a bit.'

'It's so much easier if we can go out the four of us,' she complained. 'Can't you just explain to Tom that you're a bit shy and that you want to go slow?'

'You know it's not just that,' I told her. 'I really like him and I don't want to lead him on. Besides, I'm scared of what I might do. Maybe it's best if I just leave it, at least till I can talk to him. Or . . .' I add with a wicked grin, 'maybe you'd like to tell him *for* me. Something like: "Hmm, the thing is, Tom, Julia doesn't want to get off with you, so can you just keep your hands to yourself till she feels she is ready?" . . . or maybe, "Tom, Julia is only fourteen – do you still want to go out with her?"'

By this point, Anna was holding her sides, laughing. 'OK OK, I see the problem,' she conceded, 'but let's see if we can work something out so we can still see them again. I just can't cope with the stress of trying to organise meeting Peter on my own without my parents getting all suspicious.

We did see the boys again after that for a coffee and it was fun, but I still have my doubts about me and Tom. Anna's mad about Peter and has no doubts whatsoever, even though there is definitely no chance he'll be invited to our Easter party.

'Honestly, why can't we be like other people,' we moan to each other. 'How long do we have to live in this country before our parents will accept the fact that we might go out with English boys?'

CHAPTER FOURTEEN

Cyprus in an English Garden

The aroma of suckling lamb on the spit is wafting along through all the gardens in our leafy London suburb exciting our tastebuds and filling the spring air with smoke, which is stirring up the neighbours.

'The man three houses down from us just knocked on the door to complain about the smoke,' Stavros tells everyone.

'Oh, these English. They don't know how to live,' says Andreas, one of Tony's friends. 'They just sit in their houses eating chips with vinegar! Give them some ouzo to loosen them up!'

'What's wrong with the smoke?' Mum asks in amazement when she hears about the complaint. 'It smells delicious and the worst is over anyway. The meat is nearly cooked.'

'Maybe we should invite them to join us,' says my dad in earnest.

'I don't think so,' several people protest.

If I close my eyes and breathe in the warm breeze mixed with all the different cooking aromas, I can fool myself into thinking I'm in Cyprus.

The guests have been arriving since mid-morning. Tony and Stavros's friends have volunteered to help with the cooking and basting of the lamb. So far it's been a day of brilliant sunshine and cloudless sky, and everyone is hoping it will stay that way. Anna and I are doing our dutiful daughters bit, helping our mothers with all the cooking preparations. Linda's dad dropped her off early, so she is well into the spirit of things, having rolled up her sleeves and started helping us in the kitchen. We chopped enough salad to feed an army and we made enough houmous, tzatziki and taramasalata to last a week. I was really pleased that Linda had accepted my invitation, as I wanted her to meet my family and get the chance to see how the Greeks celebrate. She has finally met Anna, and will be meeting Stella soon.

Bottles of wine, beer and ouzo have been opened and are being consumed by all the men in the traditional macho fashion as they sit or stand around the spit.

'The cooks must be well looked after,' they call out to us. 'More wine over here, girls!'

'What it is to have daughters,' I hear Dad chanting away as usual to *Kyrios* Petros in the garden. 'Girls – guaranteed to look after you!' He always says that at every opportunity and it really annoys me, even though I know he means well and is only showing his pride in having an *obedient, good* daughter, a virtue that is expected of all nice Greek girls. But why doesn't he say the same about having sons! It is such an antiquated, sexist thing to say and it really bugs me and makes me want to behave badly, which of course I don't. I just moan at Anna, whose dad is exactly the same.

A key part to the Easter ritual is the cracking of the red eggs. These are real eggs, which are hard-boiled first, then dyed crimson and sometimes decorated with patterns. They are arranged into baskets and placed in the middle of the table as a centrepiece. On Easter Sunday each person takes an egg and cracks it with someone else, by taking turns hitting the top of one egg against the other. Whichever egg survives unbroken is declared the 'lucky egg' and the owner of it, the lucky person of the year. It's a really fun tradition with lots of screaming and laughing and mock competitiveness.

While the boys are cooking, Stella, who has now arrived too, takes the basket around for everyone to choose their egg. I try to explain to Linda what this is all about, but Anna does a much better job of it.

'It's a ritual that celebrates life and the rebirth of nature, as well as the Christian thing,' she tells her, in a nutshell.

Linda thinks everything is fantastic, loves all the food, and surprise, surprise, has taken a shine to Tony.

'They're so good-looking,' she says to me in the kitchen. 'They're not like English boys at all, and haven't they all got broody eyes! You didn't tell me you had such a gorgeous brother!'

'I quite agree,' says Stella, 'but hands off – he's mine!'

'Forget it, girls,' says Anna. 'We are all too young for him. He likes them old and wrinkly. You have to be at least twenty for him to even look.' We all laugh.

'It's ready!' shout out the boys and everyone runs to help lift the meat off the spit. Once everything is laid out on the table, the feast begins. Eating, like sleeping and singing, is a very serious activity for the Greeks, so everyone throws themselves into enjoying the meal with great enthusiasm and nobody rushes their eating. Linda is visibly enjoying herself and I recognise in her expression my own feeling of belonging that I had at her brother's party.

'I like this very much,' she tells me with a mouthful of lamb. 'My grandmother cooked meat like this.' I knew she would like it and I can't wait to see her reaction to the rest of the day when the singing and dancing begins.

Halfway through the meal it is decided it's time to crack the eggs, so the usual scrum of who was going to crack with whom starts. Stella makes a beeline for Tony, who luckily is nice enough to oblige and she is delighted, even when he manages to smash her egg to bits! Linda ended up having the hardest egg and was declared the lucky one of the year and promised to take it home and keep it as a souvenir.

'Bad idea,' I tell her. 'I try it once but after a few days the egg was so disgusting and I had to throw it away.'

'So how come the Chinese have eggs a hundred years old and they are fine? I'll try it anyway,' she insists.

Once the table has been cleared and while the women, in typical Greek fashion, are dealing with the dishes, Anna's uncle picks up his guitar and starts strumming and singing. Song after song, like a human juke box, he plays and sings, and one by one everyone joins him, turning it into one, big, wonderful unifying act. It's incredible how many songs people know and how we all remember the words, even if we haven't sung them for years. I remember songs from when I was very little, even from as long ago as my mother's womb! I think music is so powerful it can stir up feelings and memories from our deep subconscious.

First we sing nostalgic ballads of lost love and lost homeland, until the mood turns more jovial and we all get up to dance. We join hands, boys and girls, mothers and fathers and friends, and we dance in the back garden of our semi-detached house under the brooding London sky, oblivious to our surroundings, as the strange music is carried like the smoke through the small patches of green gardens, to the ears of our English neighbours.

The sky gets darker and moodier as the day progresses, but ignoring it, we let our good humour carry us on with the dancing and singing, till suddenly a massive cloudburst chases us all inside. We move the tables and chairs out of the way and the party continues way into the evening with more food and drink till Linda's dad comes to pick her up.

'Ask him in for a drink,' Mum insists, and he accepts.

'No more ouzo, thank you,' he says, smiling and nodding at my brother who is trying to refill his glass. 'I'm driving.' Under the table, however, I can see his feet tapping along to the music.

'Next time we will invite all the family,' Mum tells me, pointing at my friend's dad.

CHAPTER FIFTEEN

Vine Leaves Need the Sun to Grow

'That was a lovely party,' Linda says the following week when we're back at school. We are having a food technology lesson. Our teacher, Miss Jones, is a short, fat woman who speaks like she has something hot in her mouth and is moving it around trying not to burn her tongue. The result is that I understand nothing of what she says, which makes it very difficult to follow the lesson. Today I think she is trying to show us how to make some kind of cake, judging from the flour, eggs and sugar she's got out on the table.

'My dad really liked it too,' Linda whispers, while Miss Jones is droning on.

'Other time you all come,' I whisper back, feeling proud.

These cookery lessons are a funny thing for me and bear no resemblance to the kind of cookery that I'm used to. My mother is very keen on me learning to cook and in Cyprus she always called me to come and help her or watch what she was doing. But I always wanted to be outside playing with all the other kids, not watching her fry aubergines.

'Some day you'll have to cook for your family,' she would shout to me as I ran past her, 'so come and learn to make meatballs.' That would be enough to send me dashing out of the house. But since we've been in England, I spend all my time at home, and helping with the cooking is not so bad.

Stuffed vine leaves are my favourite thing to cook and I find the whole ritual of it almost spiritual. It probably has something to do with the fact that it is a group activity. I always remember my mother making this dish with at least one other person, like one of my aunties or one of her friends. The kitchen table would be covered with an assortment of bowls and plates, full of different ingredients, either bought in the market or brought in from the garden. Pots of hot water would be boiling away on the stove, and the aroma of the chopped herbs and spices would fill the room. And the whole process is always done with plenty of laughter and good humour. Back home, my mum would send me out into the backyard in the early summer to pick the greenest, freshest, most succulent leaves on the vines. In England she buys them from the Greek shops, but when Sophia's family come to visit, she'll get them to bring some for her.

The leaves are stuffed with minced lamb mixed with rice, finely chopped onions, tomatoes and aromatic spices and herbs, such as cinnamon, dried mint, parsley, salt and pepper. First the leaves are placed in boiling water for a few minutes till they are soft, then, one by one, my mum lays a leaf on the palm of her hand and puts just the right amount of stuffing. Then, in a miraculous gesture like a conjurer, she rolls the leaf into a perfect parcel that manages to stays tightly wrapped even after an hour of cooking in a pot with lots of liquid, made up of tomatoes, lemon juice, olive oil and water. I always watch this ritual in amazement and try to imitate her, but can't manage it. I have to lay each leaf on a plate and carefully and slowly roll it into shape using both hands.

'By the time you're my age you'll be able to do it too,' she always says encouragingly. She learned by watching her mother and sisters, and I know these rituals are passed down from generation to generation. 'You too will show your daughter how to make them some day,' she tells me with a smile, and I try to imagine my mother, the youngest of eight, at my age – cooking with her mother and older sisters. When she was growing up, life was so different and primitive in our country. Cyprus at that time was almost a third world country and trying to picture it was difficult. Not all houses had running water or electricity, and certainly no fridges or cookers. They kept their food fresh in ice boxes.

'The ice man would call round at people's houses like the milkman does now,' she explained, 'and bring huge blocks of ice that we would put in a box to keep our food and drinks in. We couldn't keep things for long – it all had to be got fresh each day.'

I try and visualise myself at my mum's age with a teenage daughter and find that just as impossible to do.

In our Cookery class with Miss Jones today, it seems we are learning to make a *sponge* cake. I look up the word 'sponge' in my faithful English-to-Greek pocket dictionary, which I carry with me everywhere, and feel even more confused after I've read the definition. 'Sponge' and 'cake' don't sound very compatible to me, nor very appetising . . .

CHAPTER SIXTEEN

Waiting for Sophia

We're well into the summer term now and life seems to be much brighter somehow. The walk to school is getting better and better with each day and when I get home it's still light and I can sit in the garden and chat with Anna till late. Our plans for the summer and the family trip to Spain are also well on their way and I can hardly contain my excitement. My aunt and uncle said they might send Sophia on ahead so she can spend some time in London with us before we go to Spain. At last the two of us can be together again and I can show her what kind of life I've been having in England for the last year. She will meet my friends and I can take her to all the places I know. So much has happened since we were last together and I want to share everything with her.

'I can't wait till Sophia comes,' I tell Anna as we walk to school. 'I know you'll really like her. She is fun and a rebel and always did things when we were little that could get us into trouble, but she knows how to get out of it too.'

'We'll have to take her shopping in the West End and show her all the sights,' Anna enthuses.

'We can go on an open-air bus ride and visit the London Zoo and show her all the touristy things that people do when they come over.'

'It will be great taking her everywhere, because we know how to get about now, don't . . .'

'Definitely,' I say, cutting her short because I see my bus coming around the corner and I start running to catch it. I've been taking the bus for the rest of the way to school recently because there is a boy I see who always smiles at me. I first noticed him when I decided to jump on the bus one morning because I was a bit late. He came and sat next to me and, without saying anything, just smiled at me. He's really good-looking, and I know he goes to the boys' school, because I recognise the uniform. He's got jet-black, shoulder-length hair, which I really like. In Cyprus, long hair isn't allowed on boys, and girls have to wear theirs off their face. But in England they don't seem to mind if you have your hair long – even the boys, which looks great. He's about my age or a little bit older, very slim, but I can see he's quite muscly, with big, brown eyes, long eyelashes and dark eyebrows. He looks almost Greek. I've never even said hello to him, but I hear him talking with his friends and he has a lovely deep voice, which sounds different to the way the other boys talk. I think I have a crush on him, but I've decided to keep my distance from the opposite sex till I can actually have a conversation without an interpreter.

I'm still keeping my distance from Tom and haven't seen him much lately. We have been to the cinema with Anna and Peter a couple of times, and although he's been really sweet and not put any pressure on me, I just can't let myself relax with him. I keep thinking about what he'd say if he knew how old I was. Anna tells me that I over-analyse things and that I should go with the flow a bit more . . .

In assembly, Miss Woodcock, our headmistress – a short, thin, colourless woman with equally colourless hair, announces that the nearby police cadets' academy is having a summer party and that all the girls from our year and the years above are invited.

'That's exciting about the summer party!' Linda says during break, while we're taking our usual stroll around the school playground.

'I like the boy on the bus,' I tell her, blushing. 'He's very good-looking and he smiles at me.'

'Ooooh really! So what boy is that?' she says with mock disapproval.

'He's from the boys' school. I see him in the morning.'

'And? What are you going to do about it?'

'Nothing! He is just . . . eye-candy,' I say, trying out some new vocabulary.

'Does he have a nice friend?' Linda asks, grinning at me. 'I could do with a nice boy smiling at me . . .' and we both giggle.

Lessons are becoming much more bearable lately and I'm starting to understand a lot of what is being said in most subjects. Miss Hammond's Saturday morning lessons seem to be really helping and Dad is delighted with my progress.

'You see?' he says, feeling pleased with himself. 'You didn't want to bother, but it's done you so much good having this extra help.'

I nod in agreement because I know it's true. As much as it is a pain to give up my Saturday mornings, I know it's really helping me – and besides, I enjoy going to Miss Hammond's house and seeing her cats.

To my amazement, I've been discovering that a lot of English words are actually derived from Greek. And if I see them written down and I pronounce them phonetically, they sound completely Greek. I find this incredible, and when I tell my dad, he explains that English is one of the richest languages in the world because it is made up of so many other languages – Greek and Latin being the main ones. He also tells me that an English professor at Oxford or somewhere gave a lecture once, using only words that were derived from Greek. So, if you were to pronounce those words in the Greek way, then the lecture would have been a Greek one! I think this is a truly stunning fact and I spend considerable time amusing myself finding Greek words in everything.

'Did you know that the word "photography" is a Greek word?' I ask Linda. 'It comes from the Greek word *"photo"*, which means "light", and *"graphy"*, which means "to write". So "photography" means "to write with light",' I say triumphantly. 'Even the word "idea" is a Greek word, which means just that. Did you know that?'

'No,' she says smiling, 'I had no idea!'

I smile back because I know she's teasing me. I'm being really boring about this, but it is such a revelation for me and something of a breakthrough, possibly bordering on an obsession . . .

CHAPTER SEVENTEEN

Summer's on Its Way

Only a month to go before school finishes for the summer holidays. It's hard to believe that a whole academic year has nearly passed. In some ways, it feels as if it's gone really fast and in others it seems like a lifetime. I miss my country a lot, and my friends, my grandfather and my cousins. I miss Chloe and our house. But above all, I miss the freedom the summer brings there. We have such long holidays in Cyprus – three whole months without school! The five weeks we get here seem pathetic in comparison. I will be celebrating my first birthday since arriving in England and the fact that Sophia will be here for it almost makes up for not seeing her for a year. I don't think I could face it without her because we have always spent our birthdays together. I'm counting the days until we'll be together again.

Schools in Cyprus finish earlier than in England because of the hot summers, which make it impossible for children to concentrate on anything. The heat generally intolerable in the last few weeks of the school year and our walk home in the midday sun was always a torture. We would all drag our feet together in a big gang, stopping to rest under the shade of a tree and wiping the sweat off our dripping faces.

Most families, mine included, would escape the oppressive heat of the cities and go to cooler parts of the island for the summer holidays, either to the sea or to the mountains. My family always chose a cool mountain village for our holidays and we spend the entire three months there. The little villa we rented was completely basic with not much furniture so we would have to pile our car high with bedding, pots and pans and sometimes even a mattress was hoisted on top of our car. My mother, notorious for her lack of organisation, was always in a packing frenzy well after the scheduled time of departure and we always made most of our journey in the dark. The year I found Chloe, she was still a little kitten, so we had to take her with us because she was too young and frail to be left behind. I sat with her on my lap, stroking her to keep her from crying. Since I suffer from car sickness, the two-hour journey to the village was always punctuated with stops by the side of the road, so I could throw up, and that summer it was no different.

'You know she always gets car sick when you drive like that around the bends,' Mum said, darting accusing glances at Dad.

'I'm doing my best,' he replied, feeling guilty. 'It's not my fault the roads are bad, we *are* driving up a mountain, you know.'

At some point I decided that Chloe needed a pee. The darkness had set in by now and Dad was trying not to lose her in the dim light of the head lights while she was peeing. Of course, the inevitable happened, and an hour later he was still trying to find her in the blackness of the mountain slope. I was in floods of tears and inconsolable.

'You lost her!' I sobbed. 'You should have held her while she did it.'

'*You* should have held her while she did it,' my brother hissed at me. 'What a stupid idea anyway, to take a kitten in a car and then let her out for a pee. She is not a person, you know, in case you didn't notice.'

She was eventually found chasing a leaf around in the dark as if it was a mouse and blissfully unaware of the disruption she had caused. I scooped her up in my hands and she slept in my lap for the rest of the journey. We finally arrived in the dead of night at our villa. In the morning we found a family of scorpions nestling in Dad's shoes under the bed, which Chloe was guarding!

'So what do you want to do for your birthday?' asks Anna as we walk down the street, each holding a huge ice cream cone.

'Well,' I say with a mouthful of pistachio and chocolate, 'Sophia will be here too, so maybe we can go for a pizza and I can ask Stella and Linda too.'

'Don't you want to ask the parents if we can have a party?'

'Oh, I don't know if I want to do that. I don't think I know enough people, and besides, I've got that big summer party at the cadet school to go to.'

'OK,' she says, disappointed, as it would have been a good opportunity to see Peter.

'I'm sorry, Anna,' I say, feeling a little sorry for her. 'I know it would be fun, but just think of the stress with both sets of parents around *and* our brothers. It was fine at Stella's, because her parents were out and her brother is on her side.'

'I suppose.'

'I've got an idea, though,' I say brightly. 'This police cadet thing could be OK, and I thought I would ask if you and Sophia can come too. The whole point of inviting the girls' school is to get girls, so the more the better, I would have thought.'

'I can't ask Peter there, though, can I?'

'No, but you never know . . .' I say and give her a mischievous grin, 'you might meet a lovely policeman.'

CHAPTER EIGHTEEN

Together at Last!

I'm standing at the arrivals gate in Heathrow airport with Tony, waiting for Sophia to come through. We've already been here for half an hour and the plane has only just landed. I whined and moaned at Tony all morning about not being late in case there was traffic on the way, so we got here way too early and now it's his turn to moan at me.

'You're such a pest,' he says. 'I shouldn't have listened to you. If her luggage is late we could be here for hours.' He stalks off in a huff to get himself a drink.

But I know that he volunteered to drive me here because Sophia is also his favourite young cousin – not that he shows it much, but a gesture like this from him indicates how fond he is of her.

I hardly slept all night – I'm so excited about seeing Sophia again. When we were little we would always be thrilled to see each other after being apart for a long time. In the winter, we spent practically every day together, but in the summer she would go to the seaside with her family and we went to the mountains, so we spent the best part of three months in different places. My dad, who used to come and join us at the weekends, would sometimes bring a relative or a friend with him to spend a couple of days with us, and I always wished he would bring Sophia with him instead of the boring adults he always arrived with. Then one Friday afternoon while I was having my siesta, Mum came to wake me up. 'I have a surprise for you,' I remember her saying, and I opened the door to discover my beloved cousin standing there, smiling from ear to ear. We hugged and kissed and jumped up and down on the bed, shrieking with happiness. She stayed for two weeks with us and that was the best summer ever!

So now, standing at the arrivals gate, eyes glued to the sliding doors in case I miss her, I'm filled with the same kind of bubbling excitement as I was when I was seven, and I know that this summer will be better than ever! Ten months is a long time to have been away and the longest Sophia and I have ever been apart.

After what seems like hours, the sliding doors open, and there on her own, framed by the big glass doors, pushing a trolley piled high with luggage, is Sophia. She strolls into one of the biggest airports in the world in her usual nonchalant way, like she's done it a hundred times before. She's wearing a denim mini-skirt with a white T-shirt and she looks taller and tanned, her long hair the colour of golden honey streaked with sunshine spilling over her shoulders – tell-tale signs of time already spent in the sun. Suddenly she sees us and her face breaks into a huge smile as I run towards her, eyes blurred with tears. We fall into each other's arms, shrieking. We hug and hug and kiss and jump up and down, blocking the way for the other passengers and embarrassing Tony.

'Come on, you two,' he says, 'you can do that later.' But he's smiling.

We both sit in the back of the car, having piled the bags on the front seat beside Tony, and we talk non-stop all the way home.

'It's OK,' he says with a grin. 'Don't mind me, girls. I'll just be your taxi driver for the day.'

'Oh my God, Ioulia *mou*,' Sophia says in amazement, 'you look so grown-up and so *pale*. Your hair is darker and your face is lighter!'

'It's because we don't have any sun in this country!'

'There is lots of sun above the clouds,' she says, laughing. 'It was brilliant sunshine until the plane went through the clouds and landed!'

'Some days you don't know that there *is any* sun here, even above the clouds,' I say.

'But it's summer now. Will it be hot while I'm here? Can we go to the sea?'

'I hope so, Sophia *mou*. I really want the weather to be good for you so we can do everything and go to the sea as well if you like. I haven't seen it yet – well, not since we arrived in England on that ferry from France, but I try to blank that memory.'

'Why? What was wrong with it?' she asks.

'Well, we all threw up the entire journey and I felt so ill I can't remember anything, and if I do, I try to forget it!'

'It's true,' Tony adds from the front. 'Even I try to forget that. It was the worst.'

Everyone is waiting for us at the house (even Anna's parents are there to greet her). My mum has cooked lots of lovely food for a welcome feast. Anna and Sophia finally meet, then I can't wait to show her my clothes, shoes, make-up and tell her all about Tom and the party, and the boy on the bus – and everything that has happened to me so far. There is so much to catch up on, but we have a whole month ahead of us.

Because the house is so small Tony has arranged to stay with a friend of his so Sophia can sleep in my room for the whole time. It is bliss to be sharing my bedroom with a girl and not my brother. We stay up nearly all night talking. 'Thank God it's Saturday tomorrow,' I say to Sophia when we finally decide it's time to go to sleep.

CHAPTER NINETEEN

A New Perspective

'Do you mean that above us there are streets and cars and buses and people walking around and everything?' Sophia asks, amazed and looking around with her big brown eyes even bigger than usual. We're sitting on the tube on our way to Oxford Circus because Anna and I are taking her into town for her first visit.

'When we did this in February, there was snow everywhere,' says Anna. 'We were wearing more clothes than you can imagine. Trying to be warm and look cool at the same time is not easy!'

In total contrast, today the temperature is warm and the three of us are dressed in jeans and T-shirts with jumpers tied around our waists for later.

I feel so free! I can't believe what a difference a sunny day makes, I think and beam with pleasure to be sitting on the London Underground with my favourite cousin and best friend, actually knowing where I'm going and what I'm doing. I can read most of the signs now, even though I still have to follow Anna around the labyrinth of tunnels. I feel that soon I just might be able to do this on my own.

'Wow! It's incredible,' exclaims Sophia, shading her eyes from the sun to look up at all the tall buildings as we step onto the busy pavement. 'So many people, so many cars!' Her reaction reminds me of my own the first time I did this, and I give her a hug.

'Let's hit the shops,' I say cheerfully, 'and then let's go to that coffee bar where we met the boys. Do you think we can find it?' I ask Anna.

'We'll give it a go and if not we'll find a new one.'

London on a sunny summer's day is jumping with life and good vibes. The music spilling onto the streets from the shops in Carnaby street is infectious and it makes us want to dance while we walk along.

'I want to buy some music to take back with me,' says Sophia, walking into a record shop.

'I want to buy a bikini for Spain,' I say, following her in. 'I can't wait to jump into the sea again.'

'I couldn't imagine wearing a swimsuit ever again after this winter,' says Anna.

'I know. I thought it would never end.'

'I don't know why we couldn't find that coffee bar,' Anna says, disappointed, as a waitress shows us to our table at an open-air café, much later that day. 'I thought it was down that little side street, but everything looks so different today.'

'It doesn't matter,' I say as we take the weight off our feet, taking our seats in the evening sun. 'I prefer this place. We can sit outside, and anyway, it's good to try somewhere new.'

We walked around all morning, in and out of shops in Regent Street and Oxford Street, then down to the river, past the Houses of Parliament because Sophia wanted to see Big Ben ('Wow! It really *is* big,' she said, craning her neck to look at the big clock towering over us), past Buckingham Palace ('That's really boring,' she said. 'Seen much better palaces in Vienna when I went there with my mum.'), looked at some pigeons in Trafalgar Square, and eventually found ourselves in Covent Garden. The whole area is buzzing with activity. The market, the music, the street performers and cafés give the place an air of such festivity that it reminds us all of a village *fiesta*.

In Cyprus, especially in the summer, villages around the island celebrate the name day of their patron saint with a *fiesta* or a *paniyiri*. The village streets are turned into festive marketplaces for a few days, with stalls selling local produce, toys, jewellery and food. There is music and dancing in the streets and games played by everyone, old and young. People look forward to their village *paniyiri* because it attracts visitors from all over the island and, as children, we couldn't wait to go to them because they were the best fun. Sitting in this open-air café in the middle of London, there was a very familiar feel about the activities around us and we were having a great time.

'I love London,' says Sophia. 'It's such fun, and the weather is brilliant too.' For some reason, since the day she arrived, the sun hasn't stopped shining and the temperature has risen as well. It seems that London, for the past week, has been having a summer.

'I love London too,' I say, 'because you are here!'

As soon as I say it, I suddenly realise that I am beginning to really like living here. Sophia's visit has highlighted how much fun London can be once you get to know it – and I was definitely starting to feel more at home in this vast city.

Boy Trouble

'Never do that to me again!' I hiss at Anna after I hang up the phone, turning to look at her with a face so flushed that I'm sure I'm red and blotchy all the way down to my chest. I'm almost shaking, half with rage at Anna and half with excitement.

I was talking to Tom – well, I say talking, but of course that's not strictly true. All I really did was listen to *him* talking, while I muttered the odd word here and there in reply. I understood everything he was saying to me, and I kept wanting to reply, but the phone is not really the best means of communication when words get stuck in your mouth and thoughts and sentences are not synchronised.

Anna had been on the phone, talking to Peter as I was chatting with Sophia, when she unexpectedly handed me the receiver and walked away. I had no idea what to expect, and after a limp 'hello', I heard Tom's voice at the other end.

'Why don't you want to see me?' he asked quietly. Since Sophia arrived London, I've been avoiding Tom completely, even though Anna has carried on seeing Peter. She sneaks off to meet him for a while on her own when the three of us go into town. She keeps telling me that Tom is asking about me and wants to see me, but I really need to put some distance between us. With Sophia here, I thought it was the perfect time to do so. What the hell could I say to him on the phone, with my limited vocabulary, in the middle of the living room, and with the possibility of someone walking in on me?

'I just don't think that was very clever,' I say to Anna. 'What did you think I was going to be able to say to him? It's not like I could say, "I really like you, but I'm not ready to shag you yet", is it?'

'I'm so sorry, Ioulia *mou*,' she says apologetically, seeing how upset I am. 'You're doing so well these days – I really thought you'd be OK to talk to him. He seems so lovesick. He really wanted to talk to you.'

Hearing Tom's voice again reminded me of how much I like him, but I have made up my mind. It is too dangerous to carry on seeing him.

I look at Sophia, who's sitting on the sofa painting her nails, and I can see she is trying not to laugh.

'You heartbreaker, you!' she says to me cheekily and bursts out laughing. 'What have you done to that poor English boy?'

Suddenly the tension is gone and we all burst into hysterical laughter.

'It was just a bit of fun,' I manage to say between gasps for breath. 'It wasn't meant to get so serious . . .'

Of course I've told Sophia everything about Tom and

the party, and even though she is a daring sort of person, she agreed it was best if I cooled it off with him for now.

'It's not really the kissing and the getting off with him that bothers me,' she says now. 'It's his age. If he was the same age as us it wouldn't matter, but just think – he's the same age as Tony!'

'I know! What a thought! That's what worries me too,' I say.

'He's in a totally different stage of life. And if he finds out how old you are he'll freak, I'm sure.'

'I'll never tell him that,' I say, 'I'd rather just not ever see him again than admit I hadn't been honest about my age.'

'It's a shame,' Anna interjects. 'He's a really nice person. And from a selfish point of view, it helps me with going out with Peter!'

'I know,' I say. 'And you know, the worst thing is that I actually really like him. But it just doesn't feel right. It's bad timing, I think. If I was to meet him, like, two years from now, I think it would be different.'

'Never mind, girls,' Sophia says cheerfully. 'Let's see if we can each find a nice boy at this policeman's ball on Saturday.'

I'd asked at school if my friend and cousin could come along to the dance and was told it wouldn't be a problem. The parents are fine about it too, as the party has been organised by the school (and for some reason, they think this means it will all be very respectable!).

We all bought some nice new summer clothes on our shopping expedition, so getting ready for the party is going to be even better fun. People say that three is a bad number for friends, but we all seemed to get on really well. The fact that Anna was a bit older, and of course that she and Sophia liked each other so much, really helped.

'Do you want to come and get ready for the party at my house?' I ask Linda as we're leaving the school gates on Friday.

'Yes, please,' she says excitedly. 'Would the others mind?'

'Definitely no! Anna likes you a lot and you can meet my cousin. She doesn't speak English, but she is fun.'

'No problem there for me,' she says, smiling. 'I like foreigners, remember?'

Linda is coming part of the way home with me even though it's out of her way, because she wants to catch a glimpse of the boy on the bus.

'Is that him?' she asks, pointing at a boy with long hair who got on the bus the same time as us.

'No, not him,' I reply. 'The boy I like is very good-looking – wait and see.'

We wait, but with no luck, and Linda has to get off. 'See you tomorrow about five,' she shouts and hops off the bus, waving goodbye. I'm watching Linda through the window as she walks down the street and disappears around a corner, when I sense someone sit down next to me. I turn my head and see *him*, smiling at me – his white teeth gleaming and black hair hanging over one eye. I blush from head to toe, but manage to smile back before I turn away and look out of the window again.

CHAPTER TWENTY-ONE

Party Time!

'You missed him yesterday,' I tell Linda the next day as I'm leading her up the stairs to my bedroom. 'He must have been on the bus already. As soon as you left he came and sat next to me.'

'Well . . . ? What did he say?' she asks, but doesn't wait to hear my answer. 'Did you speak to him?'

'No, I was too shy. He didn't say anything – just smiled, and I smiled back.'

'You'll have to do more than that if you want to go out with him,' she says, grinning.

'I don't know if I want to go out with him yet. I'll wait and see,' I tell her as we reach my bedroom, where Anna and Sophia have already started to get ready for the party.

A cool summer breeze is blowing in through the open window and the loud music that we're playing to get us in the party mood is blaring out the window the other way into the garden.

I can hear my mum's voice in the garden as she drinks her coffee with *Kyria* Eva. 'It's so nice to see the girls having fun,' she says.

'It's lovely,' *Kyria* Eva replies with a little sigh. 'It reminds me of *my* youth.'

The pile of clothes on the bed, the shoes and make-up all over the floor and the smell of perfume, are all signs of the frenzied fun we are having as we decide what to wear. Part of the joy of getting ready is leisurely trying on clothes and asking each other's opinion, listening to music and laughing.

'Thanks for asking me over,' says Linda, 'It's such fun to be doing this with you three.'

Sophia is wearing a short white skirt to show off her tanned legs and a halter-neck, candy-stripe top. She takes a long time to decide which shoes to wear, but eventually ends up with a pair of knee-high suede boots.

'They're good for dancing,' she says. 'I hate being uncomfortable, and I want to dance all night tonight!'

I've gone for a pair of flared black trousers with a chunky silver chain belt and a deep purple top with a plunging neckline.

'Watch that cleavage,' Sophia teases me. 'You don't want to break any more hearts! You've done enough damage to the male population of this country already . . .'

Stupid boys, I think to myself. They are so impressionable.

Anna's wearing a summer dress with spaghetti straps, while Linda has put on a long peasant-style skirt with a pretty floral pattern and a plain black, tight-fitting T-shirt. I've been put in charge of everyone's make-up and all my practising has paid off.

Finally, made up and dressed up, we check each other out

– face, hair, clothes – and we decide that we look gorgeous. None of the boys from the police school will be able to resist any of us! Then we make our way downstairs.

'They've done it again! No one would believe their age!' Tony exclaims to Stavros, as we're waiting downstairs for Dad to get the car out of the garage. Somehow this time, even though he looks concerned, Tony seems to have resigned himself to the fact that his little sister is growing up.

'Now, remember the rules,' my dad says to me in the car. 'Don't be too familiar with any of the boys and, above all, act with dignity. Your cousin is our guest and I'm responsible for her. Your uncle will not be very pleased if anything happens.'

'Yes, yes, fine,' I say impatiently, rolling my eyes with boredom at hearing the same old lecture again. 'We know the rules, don't worry,' I reassure him, knowing perfectly well that he'll be none the wiser, whatever we do.

CHAPTER TWENTY-TWO

Dancing, Snogging and Having Fun!

The boy I'm dancing with is standing oppressively close to me. My chest is crushed up against his and because it's so hot we are practically stuck together. If he just wasn't holding me so tight, I think I'd really like dancing with him because he's just the right height and doesn't talk too much. Tall boys always give me a neck-ache from looking up at them and make me feel claustrophobic. Out of the corner of my eye I see Sophia in a similar clinch with another boy and when she catches my eye she pulls a silly face at me. I feel a giggle rising up, but I manage to suppress it. I know that Steve, my dancing partner, would think I was laughing at him, and I would definitely not be able to explain. He's been very polite and nice, apart from the close dancing, and I don't want to hurt his feelings.

When the slow dance is eventually over, we return to dancing without partners, and the four of us girls start dancing together, but the boys we were with insist on keeping close to us.

'This is such fun,' shouts Sophia. 'I love London! Can't wait to tell everyone back home!'

The live band that's playing sounds fantastic. It's the first time I've been to a party with live music that isn't a *bouzouki* band playing traditional Greek songs (except for Linda's brother's party, which was practically Greek!). The drum beat thumping right through me is intoxicating. The hall has been decorated with balloons and streamers and the huge mirrored disco ball hanging from the ceiling is reflecting rainbow colours around the room.

Dripping with sweat, we make our way to the bar for a Coke and then Steve asks me if I'd like to go out into the academy's garden for some fresh air. Lots of people are sitting on the grass in groups. I catch sight of Linda sitting with some of her other friends under a tree and she grins and gives me a wave. The cool evening breeze feels delicious and I kick off my shoes as we sit on the grass, sipping our drinks. Here we go again, I think to myself, *conversation*.

Steve asks the inevitable question. 'So, how long have you been in England?' This bit is fine, as I've done it so many times before, and I'm able to explain about where I come from, how long ago and what I'm doing here. It's when it gets to 'Will you go out with me?' and 'Why can't I see you again?' that it gets complicated.

Steve's nice to look at but not a patch on Tom or the boy on the bus. He's got short, fair hair, which is neither blond nor brown, pale skin and greenish eyes. His teeth are even and white and he smiles a lot, and I can see he's got nice strong muscles in his arms – I suppose from all the training he does, if he's going to be a policeman. But I guess that's what it is about him I don't quite like – he looks like a budding policeman! He's not in the least bit artistic-looking, or individual. He's too neat and clean. Not my type, I decide. In fact, none of the boys here tonight are my type – too many clones and not enough creativity.

'Will you come out with me, Julia?' he asks very gently.

Oh God! I think again. 'I can't go out with English boys,' I tell him. I decide this is my best excuse and hard for anyone to argue with. 'My family don't allow it.'

'But I'll look after you,' he says, surprised. 'Tell your father that I'm a policeman and I'll protect you.' He gives me a big smile.

Yeah, right, I think, that's the problem – you're a policeman! The fact is, although my father would be really angry and upset if he knew I was seeing an English boy, I know that if I liked him enough, I would find a way to persuade him. With Steve, however, as nice as he is, it wasn't enough to go through all the bother.

Back in our bedroom, Sophia, Anna and I are holding a post-mortem on the dance.

'He tried to stick his tongue all the way down to my tonsils,' Anna says, pulling a sour face. 'What is it with me and boys wanting to suffocate me with their tongue? He was obviously not a very experienced kisser – he's got a few things to learn.'

'The guy I was dancing with was a really good kisser,' says Sophia, feeling very pleased with herself. 'I've learned a thing or two this evening.'

'Well, I didn't kiss Steve, because I didn't fancy him,' I say. 'He was nice and everything, but I couldn't be bothered. I'm saving myself for the boy on the bus.'

'Oh yeah? Or a nice boy in Spain, I bet,' says Sophia with her usual wicked grin and we start laughing. All we've done since she's been here is laugh and giggle. It's been the best time I've had since coming to England.

'I'll really miss you two,' Anna says sadly. 'Just as we're having fun, you're both going to leave me!'

'You're going to be in Greece for a week anyway,' I say, 'and we'll all be back again for a few days before Sophia goes back home . . .'

'Exactly!' Sophia butts in. 'And we'd better make sure we do as much as possible before I leave!'

'We've got your birthday to celebrate yet, Ioulia,' Anna says, already feeling cheerier.

CHAPTER TWENTY-THREE

A Parallel Universe

The intensity of the heat that blasts into my face as we step off the plane takes my breath away. The Spanish sun greets us with the same ferocity as the sun in Cyprus, and the hot breeze that is blowing like a giant fan makes me feel as if I'm home at last. I'd almost forgotten this feeling. I haven't felt heat like this for a year and it makes me want to cry with joy.

'Wow, this is fantastic!' I scream to Sophia at the top of my lungs to be heard above the noisy jet engines.

'I can't believe it!' she yells back. 'It's as hot as Cyprus!'

'I know. I didn't think anywhere was as hot as Cyprus!'

Our families are way behind us, walking slowly down the steps from the plane. We are already at the front of the queue, eager to get on the bus and into the terminal. There is no time to lose – we have so much to see and so much to experience. Apart from the heat, the first thing that hits me about this region in southern Spain is the landscape, which looks incredibly familiar. In the distance, all around the airport, mountain ranges are visible, and I instantly recognise the vegetation. Oh my

God, I think to myself, I love Spain and I've only just got off the plane.

'What do you think?' I ask Sophia excitedly once we're in the terminal, queueing to go through passport control.

'I don't know yet,' she says. 'We've just got here.'

As we push our trolleys to the nearest taxi rank outside the building we are once more engulfed in the familiar embrace of the midsummer sun and I hear my uncle trying to negotiate a ride with a taxi driver in a mixture of English, Greek and Spanish.

'*Por favor, señor,*' he's saying to the man, 'San Pedro? How far?' My uncle turns around to face us, pointing at two taxis, and then beckons us to get into them. There are so many of us and we have so much luggage that we look more like a bus load of tourists on a group excursion than members of the same family. We need at least two vehicles or a bus to transport us anywhere. Sophia and I get into one of the taxis, hoping we'll have it all to ourselves. No such luck, as we end up with my brother and one of her sisters. Katerina and Maria, Sophia's sisters, are even older than Tony. The three of them get on brilliantly and the girls love my brother but always ignore us, which is OK with us because we know they'll keep Tony off our backs.

Palm trees, olive groves, eucalyptus trees and bougainvillaeas all flash by the taxi's windows as we make our way to the hotel. The road curves gently along the sides of hills and fields, and the scenery all around me is so much like home. Suddenly, as the taxi turns sharply to the right, we are faced with a breathtaking view of the Mediterranean sea in all its watery, dazzling glory. Shimmering in the summer sunlight, it stretches in front of us, merging with the sky in a scene of endless blue. My heart skips a beat at this vision and I burst into spontaneous, happy laughter.

'Look, everyone, the sea!' I exclaim, just like I used to as a child whenever we headed for the seaside. For months we would wait for the first hot spell and our first swim of the year. As soon as the warm weather arrived, we would rush home after school and my dad would take a car full of cousins and make a beeline for the coast. The sight of the sea appearing through the mountains would always fill me with a sense of happiness and optimism.

Our first visit to the English seaside (only a few weeks ago at Sophia's request) was completely different and a very disappointing affair. My dad offered to take us to Brighton as we hadn't yet ventured there, so Sophia, Anna, Stella, Linda and I squeezed into the car for a day trip.

'Look, girls, the sea,' Dad said, echoing my usual excitement, as we approached the promenade. Apart from Linda, none of us recognised the grey-green expanse of water that spread out before us.

'Where?' Sophia asked, looking around.

'There,' Dad told her, pointing in front of us.

'Why is it that colour?' I asked in amazement, thinking it looked more like a river.

'The sea reflects the colour of the sky,' Dad explained to us, and we all looked up at the sky which was a mass of grey cloud. The greyness was so depressing there. Somehow in London it is less noticeable when it is contrasted with the colours that make up the city – the buses, the cars, the advertising posters, the buildings and all the people seem to detract a bit from the lack of light and sun. But at the seaside, it is magnified a hundred times. The grey of the sky reflected in the sea looks truly grim.

'Well, there is no way I'm swimming in *that*,' I said and everyone agreed with me.

This Spanish sea, however, glistening in the sun and under a blue sky, is the sea we know and love – the sea we want to dive into, body and soul, and feel its salty embrace around us. We all know this sea because it's in our blood. I can't wait to strip down to my new bikini and jump straight into it.

'Where are we?' I ask, smiling. 'Have we come to Cyprus?

'It *is* a bit confusing,' Tony says, and everyone laughs.

Our hotel is in a little village called San Pedro. It's small and cheap, but clean, and very close to the beach. Sophia and I had fantasies of pretending to be rich and famous and staying in a five-star hotel with a swimming pool and bell-boys wearing white gloves and uniforms. But instead we have to make do with what our parents can afford, which is actually a pretty special treat anyway.

The two of us are sharing a room on the third floor with a little balcony that overlooks a small apartment block. As soon as we arrive, we throw open the French windows and step out onto the balcony, where we find we can see directly into the apartment opposite, straight into the family's kitchen. The girls in the family are busy laying the table for dinner. A red and white checked tablecloth covers the dining room table and the plates and glasses are carefully arranged. One of the girls is cutting chunky slices of bread from a large round loaf and I can see olive oil, olives, red wine and salad being carried to the table. I can hear them talk and feel I know what they are saying because I recognise the sounds and the gestures they are making, even though I don't understand a word. It's a strange sensation, this feeling of familiarity, as if I'm watching Sophia and me in that room. The girls are acting exactly the way we would.

Below, we can see a busy road, which, in the early evening, is already buzzing with life.

'Quick, let's change and go down there,' Sophia says to me and we start to unpack our suitcases.

CHAPTER TWENTY-FOUR

Latin Charm

Showered and dressed, we are sitting in a café beside our hotel, sipping Cokes, people-watching, and waiting for the others to arrive.

'Oh my God,' Sophia whispers, 'the boys are *gorgeous* in this country! Look at that one on the scooter!'

'He's going to fall off it if he carries on staring at us,' I say, laughing.

Two boys are leaning up against a wall across the street and seem to be looking in our direction as well. They've been there since we sat down. They look very intense.

'What do you think they are doing, those two?' asks Sophia. 'What are they looking at?'

'Us . . . You, I think,' I reply.

'What do you think they want?'

'I don't suppose they want anything,' I tell her. 'They're just looking.'

'Oh no! One of them is crossing the road – I hope he's not coming over here,' she says, leaning towards me and trying to look the other way.

We watch him hold his hand up to the traffic and walk

slowly across the street, smiling and holding a white rose, which we saw him pick from an obliging bush spilling over the wall. He heads straight for our table, then he leans over and hands the flower to Sophia.

'*Señorita*, for you,' he says with a little bow, white teeth and dark eyes flashing. I think he's going to kiss her hand or something and I feel a giggle coming on.

'*Gracias*,' she replies, cool as anything, and accepts the flower with a smile. Then he turns around and, stopping the traffic with his hand again, walks back to his friend.

'Oooh, *gracias*!' I tease and we both collapse into girlie giggles.

'Who was that?' we hear my brother's stern voice call from behind us. We turn around to see him approaching our table.

'No idea,' I snap at him.

'Then you shouldn't be talking to strangers,' he says, frowning.

'Oh, Tony, don't be so boring,' Sophia says to him with a smile. She's always been able to say things like that to my brother and get away with it. 'It was just a boy. We didn't do anything, it's just a bit of fun – loosen up,' she teases him.

'You might say that, young lady,' he says in his usual patronising manner, 'but these Latin types take liberties if you let them. So watch it!'

'And he should know!' she whispers into my ear.

My first night in southern Spain is a revelation for me. To be filled with a sense of familiarity in a place I have never seen before stands in complete contrast to the feeling of displacement and alienation I felt when I first arrived in England. The warm summer's night breeze, scented with the sweet smell of jasmine lining the narrow streets of the village as we walk leisurely around in search for a restaurant, feels like a caress on my skin. The scene I witnessed earlier in the apartment opposite our hotel room, the sound of music spilling out of bars into the street, the glimpses through open doors of families eating or watching TV, the children's voices and laughter as they play in the streets, all combine to create a parallel universe in which I'm totally at ease. I see a family that have taken their table out onto the pavement for their supper enjoying the night air, oblivious to anyone walking by. The old grandmother is rocking a baby to sleep and two little girls are playing with their dolls by her feet.

'It's just like Cyprus,' I say to Sophia, feeling my throat tighten with emotion. I link arms with her as we stroll along. I never imagined there were other places in the world like the one I grew up in.

CHAPTER TWENTY-FIVE

Friends Reunited

'I really missed you,' Anna tells me and she gives me the biggest welcome-home hug as I stumble out of the taxi from the airport. 'It feels like you've all been gone for months. I'm so glad you are back.' She picks up one of the bags, and follows me into the house. 'I had the worst holiday!'

'Why? What went wrong?' I ask, as I put my suitcase down in the hall and we head into the kitchen.

'Well, for a start, my aunt's house in Athens is in the centre of town, miles away from the beach, and it was, like, over a hundred degrees with no air conditioning. You couldn't walk anywhere till the sun went down, and then . . .' she carries on in a barrage of words without pausing for breath, '. . . she wouldn't let me go out on my own because she thought it wasn't safe, and those cousins of mine are such a couple of whining little brats, and everyone else I know there and tried to call had gone off to some island or other because, of course, they know what a hell-hole Athens is in the summer . . . So it was *not* the best holiday,' she finally states, then takes a deep breath. 'And how was *your* holiday?' She looks at me and Sophia with folded arms and raised eyebrows.

'You poor thing, Anna *mou*, you should have come with us,' I say and give her a hug. 'We had a brilliant time!'

'I'm glad for you. I wish I *had* gone,' she says, feeling sorry for herself. 'You must tell me all about it later, but right now I want us to make plans for this week, and where we're going for your birthday. I've been climbing the walls. I need to have some FUN before the summer is over!'

I can't believe it's my birthday next week and I'm going to be fifteen! I have already been in England for almost a year, and now I'm a year older, and most definitely a year wiser. Last year, I celebrated my fourteenth birthday floating on the Mediterranean, aboard the ship that was taking us to our new life and our new home, but it was far from the exciting cruise-liner adventure that I had been promised; it was a miserable experience, what with feeling seasick and wanting to throw up most of the time. All I could think of was the fact that I was leaving everyone I cared about behind, and sailing into a dark unknown.

I had wanted to have a party for my fourteenth birthday and Sophia and I had been making plans for it since the previous Christmas. The news of our summer departure was devastating in more ways than one. Her dad would never allow her to have her own party, so it was down to me to provide the excitement. Sadly, it was not to happen, and I ended sharing my birthday with a bunch of strangers on a boat.

My mum had arranged for the ship's band to play 'Happy Birthday' that evening in the dining room, and for the chef to bake me a suitably sickening cake. The captain, who knew my dad through his new job with the shipping company, stood up in front of everyone at dinner and proposed a toast 'to the lovely young lady who is sailing to a new life in a new land, blah, blah, blah . . .' I know it was ungrateful of me not to be more cheerful, and I felt sorry for my poor mother, but I just couldn't be happy. All I wanted was to be back home with my friends.

But I already knew my fifteenth birthday was going to be as different to the last one as England was to Cyprus! I would have my favourite cousin with me and my new friends. It was summer, I had a tan and the sun was shining most days. And London was beginning to have some appeal at last. The best thing about the English summer is that it never gets dark – well, not till late anyway. In hot countries like Cyprus and Spain, you wait for darkness to give you relief from the heat, but in England, because it's never that hot, it's a bonus to be able to stay out for so long – providing it's not raining, of course. The long days and short nights also meant that my parents were less worried if we stayed out later.

'Since you want to go for pizza, let's go to the one with the garden,' Anna suggests, 'so we can sit outside.'

'And we can pretend we are in Spain,' I say, turning to Sophia.

'No gorgeous Spanish boys, though,' she says with a sigh.

Sophia flirted with a different boy every day while we

were in Spain and she was experiencing withdrawal symptoms.

'You never know, you might meet a gorgeous Italian waiter there,' I say with a giggle.

Since Sophia's arrival, my bedroom has become more girlie. We have banished Tony's books and records and other junk by pushing them under the bed. My aunt, uncle, and Sophia's sisters have been staying in a little hotel nearby, so we've been left well alone, which has been great!

We've got all the windows open and the fan blowing at full speed, because Sophia has decided that tonight, on my fifteenth birthday, she and I are going to smoke a cigarette.

I'm feeling really anxious. 'What if someone walks in?'

'Just relax,' she says. 'No one will.'

'I don't know . . .' I say nervously. 'Why don't we wait till we go out?'

'It might make you feel sick,' Sophia says. 'It's better if we do it here the first time.' She starts rummaging through her handbag and pulls out a packet of ten Marlborough Lights.

'When did you get those?' I ask in amazement.

'When you weren't looking, obviously,' she replies with a wicked grin. 'Now, let's see,' she says, putting the cigarette in her mouth and diving into her bag again to fish out a bright green Bic lighter, which she uses to light the cigarette. 'Now, come over here and stand in front of me and look in the mirror,' she instructs.

Still holding the cigarette elegantly between her fingers, Sophia brings it up to my mouth, while I watch us in the mirror. 'Now inhale,' she says.

I take the tip of the cigarette between my lips and gingerly take a little drag, but instantly let it out.

'No, no,' she says, 'you have to inhale – take it down to your lungs, hold it a moment and then exhale. Like this . . .' She demonstrates. 'OK? Now, try again.'

'When the hell did you learn to smoke?' I ask, incredulous.

'On the last day of term. We all did it. We went to Elena's house with some of the boys and one of them had a packet of cigarettes, so we all had a go. It was great! I decided it was about time you tried it too.' She gives me one of her cheeky smiles. 'You seem to have tried everything else!'

She brings the cigarette to my lips again and this time I pull hard taking in a lungful of smoke. It instantly makes me choke.

Coughing and spluttering, eyes streaming, I give up. 'I'll stick to kissing boys, thank you. Less dangerous for my health!' I say and start spraying perfume all around the room.'

'What have you two been doing in here?' asks Anna, walking into the room.

'Sophia's been trying to lead me astray as usual, but this time she hasn't succeeded,' I reply, turning up the music really loud.

CHAPTER TWENTY-SIX

Coming-of-Age

It's a beautiful August evening, and at half past seven, the London sky is a water-colour blue. The sun is nowhere near setting yet and as the six of us walk through the park, the birds are making as much noise as us, frantically flying from tree to tree. It's the first time I've seen both Linda and Stella since before our trip to Spain. Stella has been to Cyprus with her parents and Linda to Italy with hers, so there is a lot to catch up on.

'Do you mind if Peter joins us for coffee afterwards?' Anna asks me pleadingly as we walk to the restaurant. 'I told him we're going out and he asked if he could come and see us,' she continues, looking at me with big, puppy-dog eyes.

'I hope you didn't tell him it was my birthday,' I reply in a panic.

'No, I just said we were going out because your cousin is leaving. I know you don't want them to know how old you are.'

'For God's sake, Ioulia,' Sophia butts in. 'You're not

supposed to be lying about your age until you are at least twenty-five! Pull yourself together!'

'You just be quiet and keep out of this,' I tease her back. 'I've got my reasons.'

This teasing has been going on in Greek, and since Linda doesn't understand what we're saying, I translate. Then suddenly I realise that *I'm* doing the translating instead of Anna! I can't believe how far I've come!

The walled garden of the restaurant is really pretty and the potted plants and trellises placed all around give it a very Mediterranean feel. We have a large round table in the middle of the terrace and Anna, Sophia, Linda and Stella make a big fuss by producing cards and presents and making me feel very special. There are no gorgeous Spanish waiters around, but there are some equally gorgeous Italian ones instead, who are also making a bit of a fuss of me.

I'm acutely aware of how different this birthday is to past birthdays, and it feels like a sort of coming-of-age celebration. Many changes have taken place in me. I'm sitting confidently in a London restaurant, surrounded by my new friends *and* my cousin, whom I have known and loved all my life, and I feel totally at ease. I also feel something else, which I can only describe as pride. I suddenly remember my grandfather, standing on the dock and waving goodbye to us a year ago, and I think that he would be proud of me too if he saw me sitting here like a sophisticated young woman, out with her friends in a foreign city in a foreign land, chatting away in two languages. That thought makes me happy.

'Next year we're definitely going to Italy,' Sophia is saying jokingly to everyone, just as I notice Anna's face suddenly go very pink. I follow her gaze to find Peter at the door of the terrace, searching for us with his eyes . . . and standing behind him, I see Tom! I feel my stomach lurch and my knees go weak as the two start heading for our table. I get the same sinking feeling I got when Anna handed me the phone and Tom was on the other end. I meet her gaze and her face is filled with panic, which I assume must be in anticipation of my reaction.

'Oh shit!' I whisper under my breath and give her a look that speaks volumes.

'Who are they?' whispers Sophia.

'It's Tom and Peter. Don't you *dare* tell them it's my birthday,' I hiss at everyone and quickly hide my gifts and cards in my bag under the table.

'Oops . . .' says Stella.

The boys are now standing by our table, smiling and looking even more handsome than before. 'Can we join you?' they ask politely.

'Would you like some more chairs, *signoritas*?' a waiter says, smiling conspiratorially at the boys. After everyone is introduced, Tom comes and sits next to me and Peter sits next to Anna.

Great. That's all I need, I think. I'm feeling all churned up seeing Tom again. I made such an effort to try and distance myself form him, but this is just stirring it all up again. Sitting close, he puts one arm around my chair, then leans over and starts speaking softly and slowly to me. I find the way he's talking a little irritating – it sounds really slow and precise. I also realise that I understand pretty much everything he's saying, and can reply without Anna's help.

Tom pulls back a little in surprise and stares at me with those blue eyes. 'So, do you understand everything I say now, Julia?' he says with a serious expression, but smiling with his eyes.

'Yes, I think I do,' I reply. The realisation gives me goosebumps.

'Well, it didn't take you long, did it?' he says, giving me a huge grin.

CHAPTER TWENTY-SEVEN

Tearful Goodbyes

Sophia and I have been clinging to each other for what seems like an eternity at the departures gate at the airport, and we're refusing to let go. The rest of her family are beginning to get agitated as they stand, passports in hand, waiting to go through. We were both very tearful in the car, and although my parents have told me I can spend next summer in Cyprus, it feels such a long way away. Right now, though, I'm so inconsolable that Dad promises that I can spend Christmas with Sophia this year too.

'I wish I could just stop time and hold it forever,' Sophia said to me earlier, when we were getting dressed in my room. 'I loved being here with you, but it's just gone so quickly. Why can't things last longer?'

We did have the best summer and her visit, apart from being great fun, had enabled me to appreciate London, by seeing things through her eyes – the eyes of a visitor and not of an immigrant. I had spent so long filled with disappointment and longing for what I had left behind. But Sophia found everything so thrilling and new, and her excitement was infectious.

'Come on, girls. Christmas is going to be here soon enough,' my aunt chirps.

'You've had such a great time together – just be happy about that,' says Katerina. 'You'll soon be together again.' With that she gently takes Sophia by the hand and the whole family start walking away towards departures.

'I wish she could have stayed here,' I say to my parents in the car on the way home. 'We could go to school together.'

'Maybe when she finishes secondary school in Cyprus,' Dad replies, 'she can stay with us and go to university here.'

Strange, I think to myself. I didn't say I wanted to go with her to Cyprus, I said I wanted her to stay here with me . . . I sit in the back of the car quietly contemplating what my dad has just said. I find his words very comforting and a feeling of optimism floods through me. The thought of waiting three years till we finish school doesn't fill me with gloom as I would have expected, especially as I know I'll be in Cyprus in a few months for Christmas. So, instead I try to imagine what it would be like for the two of us living as university students in London. I decide it would be great.

'I think it would be good if we move before Ioulia goes back to school.' My mother's words bring me out of my daydreaming and I start listening in on my parents' conversation from the back seat. 'It will give us some time to get the place together while she's still on holiday.'

I obviously missed this little piece of information, being so preoccupied all summer. Honestly! My parents! They're always making decisions that affect us all, but they never ask what we think about it. I wonder if my brother knows about this. I hope I don't have to change school again . . . and what about Anna? I'll miss her terribly. When I have kids I will *always* ask their opinion, I think, and feel a sulk coming on.

'When did you decide to move?' I ask moodily.

'Well, we've been thinking about it for a while,' Dad replies.

'It's so cramped where we are now,' Mum adds, 'and it's about time you and Tony had your own bedrooms. It's not fair to expect you both to share any more.'

OK, that's not a bad point. I've been happy living with Anna and her family, but I also really enjoyed not having to share a room with Tony this whole summer, and I've been wondering how it would work out when we had to start sharing again. And for months my poor brother wouldn't even come into the room until I was asleep, so it was difficult for both of us. Maybe this house move was not such a bad idea after all. But it would have been nice if we could have talked about it first and if they'd taken us to look at the place before it was all finalised. *They've* obviously been to see it, so why couldn't we all go?

'Where is the new house?' I ask my parents, feeling slightly better.

'It's not a house, actually,' Dad explains. 'It's a flat in Hampstead.'

'And are there lots of Greeks around?' I nudge my mum from the back teasingly.

'I don't think so,' she replies, 'but I can jump on the bus and go and visit people now.' I realise suddenly that she too has come a long way in a year.

132

'Please don't tell me I have to change schools or anything like that again . . .' I say pleadingly.

'Of course not,' Dad replies. 'Your school's not far – you'll just jump on the tube. It's only a few stops on the Northern Line.'

'Is the flat near the Heath?' I ask, suddenly feeling much happier about everything. Hampstead Heath was one of our favourite places to hang out this summer. We spent loads of time walking and shopping and sitting at the cafés so I got to know it well.

'Just across the street.'

'I'm really sorry you're moving,' Anna says sadly. 'I'll miss you more than you can imagine.'

'We'll meet every weekend and you can come and stay the night,' I say consolingly, 'and we'll be right in the middle of Hampstead!'

'I know, but who am I going to watch television with in the evenings?' she asks, giving me a sad smile.

'You won't be watching any television in the evenings this year – you'll be too busy revising.'

'Oh God! Don't remind me!'

Anna is going to be taking her A-levels this year and getting ready for university. She has decided she's going to study Law and things were suddenly turning very serious.

'You can arrange to meet Peter in Hampstead . . .' I suggest, trying to cheer her up – and it seemed to do the trick.

'I suppose you're right. I'll look forward to the weekends instead.'

'You can also help us move in,' I say cheerfully. 'I think they want to do it next week before school starts.'

We manage to fit half of our belongings in the back of my dad's car and the other half in Anna's dad's car, and between them, Tony and Stavros are doing the moving.

The new flat, which is just off Hampstead High Street, within walking distance from all the shops and cafés, is a big Victorian corner house, which has been converted into three flats. We have the top floor, which is flooded with light, and all the rooms look out onto the garden or our tree-lined street. I was ecstatic! My bedroom has a massive window that frames a huge plane tree and the branches and leaves seem to come straight into the room. I have my own wall-to-wall wardrobe and a dressing table.

'It is so fabulous!' Anna says to me as we are unpacking my things in my bedroom. 'You are so lucky! I think I'm going to move in with you . . .'

CHAPTER TWENTY-EIGHT

Making Sense

I'm sitting in assembly next to Linda and listening to Miss Woodcock's gentle voice welcoming us back after the summer holidays. It's the first day of school and the start of a new academic year, and I find that instead of drifting into my usual catatonic trance, I'm actually listening to her words and I understand what she is saying.

While I was getting dressed for school earlier this morning, I found, to my great surprise, that I was feeling excited about going back. I was really looking forward to it. The sense of dread and desperation I felt a year ago when I was venturing into the unknown was replaced with a sense of happy anticipation.

Sitting in assembly, I'm overwhelmed with emotion and I start to feel a tightness in my throat, I'm not sure exactly why. I look around the hall at all the familiar faces of the girls and remember how frightened I was of them and how hostile I thought they were less than a year ago. I turn around and look at Linda's profile, her dark hair falling in soft waves around her face, tanned from her trip to Italy, and I'm flooded with a sense of well-being and of love for my friend. She has been so kind and welcoming, and has given me so much support and friendship. She has made all the difference to me. I wonder what it would have been like if we hadn't become friends. I glance at the other girls too and think they are not so bad either. Linda, aware that I've been looking at her, turns to face me and gives me a big, broad, encouraging smile.

'You're a bit sad because your cousin's gone, aren't you?' she says on the way to class.

'No, I'm not sad. I'm going to see her at Christmas anyway,' I reply. 'Actually, I'm really happy,' I add realising that Linda misinterpreted my expression earlier. 'It's really strange. It might be that I'm going home soon and I'll see all my relatives and everything, but for some reason I'm really happy and pleased to be back at school. Do you think I'm weird?'

'Most definitely!'

'I understood everything Miss Woodcock droned on about,' I tell her, 'and all the chit-chat around me too. I can't tell you what this means to me, Linda. Finally, I can hear!'

We walk into the classroom where Miss Hammond, whom I carried on seeing during the holidays up until we went to Spain, is waiting for us.

'Hello, girls!' she says cheerfully. 'I hope you all had a good summer. How was Spain, Julia?'

'It was brilliant, thank you, Miss Hammond. How was your holiday in Greece?' I ask her confidently, and all the girls turn to look at me in amazement.

* * *

The best thing about moving house, apart from having my own bedroom, is the fact that I can travel most of the way home on the bus with the long-haired boy I like. A few days into the first week of term, he comes and sits next to me on the bus. I didn't see him all summer long, and when he flashes his pearly white smile at me, my heart skips a beat. He looks taller and darker than he did the last time we met, and his hair is blacker than a raven's.

'Hi!' he says cheerfully, like we're old friends. 'Did you have a nice summer?'

'Yes thanks, did you?' I reply, trying to sound as cool and casual as he is.

'I did. I went home to see my grandparents.'

'Where's that?' I ask, surprised to hear him say he went home, since I thought London *was* his home.

'Iran. We come from Tehran and my grandparents still live there,' he explains.

Iran! That's Persia, I think and then take a long look at him, and suddenly I realise that of course he is not English! Dark hair, dark eyes, dark skin – I kept thinking he was an English boy who looked Greek or Spanish, but no – he's Iranian! I know all about Persia. I learned all about the Persians and the Ancient Greeks fighting battles at school in Cyprus.

'Where do *you* come from?' he asks me, and I realise he must have known the whole time that I wasn't English either.

'I'm Cypriot,' I tell him. 'Greek Cypriot from Cyprus. Do you know where that is?'

'My parents have some Cypriot friends. They're

Turkish, I think, or Greek – I'm not sure – or both?' he says and laughs at himself. 'What's your name?'

'Julia. What's yours?' I ask. I can't believe I'm sitting on the bus, having a casual conversation with a boy I really like, with no one to translate for me.

'Nima. It's my grandfather's name. Julia sounds English to me. Do you have a Greek name too?'

'Well, in Greek it's Ioulia, but no one could say it, so I had to change it when I came over.'

'How long have you been in England?'

'Just over a year.' A voice in my head keeps telling me it can't actually be me talking with such ease.

'Is it my imagination or is it true that you couldn't speak much English a few months ago?'

'You're right. I couldn't speak any English at all when I first came,' I tell him. 'But a few months ago, I could understand a lot but was too shy to talk to anyone I didn't know.'

'I wanted to talk to you then,' he tells me, 'but you kept looking away when ever I tried.'

'Sorry. I was worried you'd ask me something I couldn't reply to.' I give him a shy smile. 'Did you speak English when you first came over?' I ask.

'I was born in England,' he explains, 'so I speak English – and Farsi.'

'Do you have the same alphabet as the English in Farsi?' I ask him.

'No, it's completely different. I speak much better Farsi than I write and read. My mum teaches us at home, but I always try to get out of it.' He looks out of the window suddenly. 'Don't you need to get off the bus soon?' he asks, remembering that I used to stay on the bus for just a few stops.

I explain that since we moved house, not only do I stay on this bus for a long time, but I have to catch a tube as well.

'That's fine by me,' he says with a smile. 'I have to catch the tube too. Which stop do you get off at?'

'Hampstead. You?'

'I get off at Belsize Park, which is the stop after,' he says, grinning. 'So you can practise your English with me every day.'

CHAPTER TWENTY-NINE

The Real Thing

'You won't believe it!' I squeak down the phone at Anna, as soon as I get home from school after meeting Nima. I couldn't wait to share my excitement with her (and then Stella, who has made me promise that I will always phone her the moment something exciting happens). 'His name is Nima. He's Iranian – and he only lives down the hill! Oh my God, Anna, I think I'm in love.'

'Honestly, you are impossible!' Anna teases me. 'I hope this one lasts a bit longer than the others . . .'

'This is the real thing – and *excuse* me, what exactly do you mean? How many others have there been? But Anna, I promise you, wait till you meet him. He's gorgeous and he's funny and intelligent and everything.'

'Does he know how old you are?' she asks, giggling.

'I'm not worried about that, because we're about the same age. Or he might be sixteen – just right.'

Anna sighs down the phone. 'Poor Tom . . . You'd better do the right thing and put him out of his misery now.'

I know I have to do something about Tom, because it

isn't really fair on him. Even though I keep putting off meeting him, we've been talking on the phone quite often. I just haven't been able to bring myself to break it off completely. I think it's because I really do like him, and it's really flattering to have a boy the same age as my brother interested in me.

'Nima asked me to go to the cinema on Saturday,' I say, avoiding the topic of Tom, 'but first I thought I'd wait till I get to know him a bit better . . .'

The next day after school I have the same excitable discussion with Linda, who is determined to come on the bus to see him.

'Maybe he'll come and talk to you while I'm still on the bus this time,' she says while we are getting our tickets.

'I'm sure he will, he says he's going to talk to me every day now. I'll introduce you to him.'

We board the bus and take a seat upstairs near the back. 'Does he have a nice friend I might like?' Linda asks with a grin. During the summer Linda saw quite a bit of the boy she met at the police cadet dance. She liked him, but she was still open to other possibilities.

'There he is!' I say pointing Nima out to Linda as he's queueing to get on the bus with a group of boys from his school.

'The one with the long hair?' she asks, which is pretty obvious, since all I've gone on about since I've met him is his long hair.

Nima eventually gets on the bus with one other friend and they both come and sit with us.

'This is my friend Linda,' I tell him, and he also introduces his friend whose name is Ali.

'Are you Turkish?' I ask him. 'My mum's best friend's son is called Ali and they're Turkish.'

'No, my family's from India,' he explains. 'It's a pretty common Muslim name.'

I look at the four of us and I'm struck by the fact that here we are, chatting away, four kids, from four different ethnic backgrounds – and who knows how many more people from different backgrounds there might be on this bus. Only a year ago, I'd never met anyone who wasn't Cypriot, and now I'm friends with kids from cultures I'd only ever read about. The expression 'melting pot' suddenly makes a lot of sense.

'So, have you decided? Will you go to the bonfire party with Nima?' Linda asks me during another brain-numbing cookery lesson. It's two months to Christmas and apparently if you are going to make a Christmas cake you have to start thinking about it now! I can't think of anything more boring than that, so, instead, we entertain ourselves by talking about boys.

'Will you *please* pay attention?' Miss Jones says sternly and we try to listen. I can't believe that Christmas will be here in two months and that I'll be in Cyprus again after all this time. I think about seeing all my family and friends and going to parties and visiting all the places I haven't seen for over a year and my heart flutters with excitement and anticipation. The way time is flying by I'll be there for my summer holidays before long! I have so much to look forward to at the moment, but most of all right now I'm looking forward to going to the party with Nima next Saturday.

It's Guy Fawkes' night on the 5th of November, and everyone is talking about going to bonfire parties, with fireworks and baked potatoes– something that passed me by completely last year. Nima explained to me on the bus that it is an annual English tradition and he has asked me to go to a party with him.

In the couple of months since school started, the two of us have spent a lot of time together. We meet most afternoons after school and travel together practically the whole way home. It's dark by the time we are out of the tube, and Nima walks me almost to my house and then the rest of the way home, which is only down the hill. As the winter darkness closes in we are becoming less shy with each other and I'm starting to relax and feel cocooned by the darkness of the streets, shielding us against the rest of the world. We started walking closer to each other, and when he took my hand one evening I didn't pull away in fear that someone would see us.

'Yes, I will go,' I whisper to Linda so Miss Jones can't hear. 'I think it'll be fun.'

'Is Anna going to go too?' she whispers back.

'No, she is too busy studying – why don't you come?'

'I don't want to be a gooseberry!'

'I think Ali's coming.'

'I don't want him to think I'm after him,' she says, and then we both shut up, as we see Miss Jones's bulky frame waddling towards us with threatening intentions.

'I can pick you up from your house and we'll go to the party together,' Nima says to me on the way home.

'I know you'll think this is strange, but my parents don't like me going out with boys – especially ones that aren't Greek,' I tell him, feeling embarrassed by my confession.

'I understand,' he says gently. 'My parents are the same with my sister. She's older now, so she puts her foot down, but when she was younger there were always dramas about going out.'

I look at him in amazement. I always assumed that only Greek girls had problems with this sort of thing.

'My dad was really against her going out with anyone, no matter what nationality,' he continues, smiling. 'He's really old-fashioned, but she is such a strong personality, he soon had to learn. If it would help, I could come and meet your parents some time.'

'Mama,' I ask that evening as I'm helping her with the dishes. 'Would you mind if I had a boyfriend?' I had been thinking about what Nima said all through dinner, but I wanted to talk to my mum about it first.

'What kind of boy?' she asks, looking at me with a worried expression.

'A really nice boy, Mama. You would really like him.'

'Is he English?'

'No, he's not.'

Her face lights up. 'A Greek boy?'

'No, Mama, he's not Greek.'

The worried expression returns. 'Not Greek? What is he, then?'

'Iranian.'

'What?'

'*Persis*,' I tell her in Greek, because I know she knows what that is, 'but only now Persia is called Iran, remember?

'Oh, *Persis*!' she says, and she looks relieved. Knowing how her mind works, I realise that in the brief moment before she answered, she remembered what she'd learned at school and connected the two nations through their ancient histories and cultures. For centuries the Persians and the Greeks were locked in a love–hate relationship, and they have a shared past of wars and battles, victories and defeats. She has decided, I'm sure, that Persians are fine, because they share so much history and culture with us.

'So, is it OK then? Can I invite him home for you and Papa to meet him?' I ask her.

'I'll talk to your father later,' she says. Then she wants to know all about how I met this Persian boy. I'm relieved, and happy to tell her, because I don't want to keep Nima a secret anymore.

CHAPTER THIRTY

Emotional Explosion

'He's only a boyfriend!' My parents and brother are all cross-examining me about Nima during dinner the next evening. 'I'm not going to marry him or anything. I'm only fifteen!'

'Yes, but we want to be sure you understand about these things, because once you start going out with a boy, there are implications,' my dad says in a solemn, serious voice.

Oh God, I knew there was a reason I kept it all to myself before, I think. I try not to get annoyed. 'Yes, yes, I know. Don't worry, I'm a sensible girl and he is a nice boy from a nice family and he will respect me.' I say, trying to appease them. 'You have nothing to worry about – really. Wait till you meet him.'

Finally, we agree that Nima can come on Saturday before the party to pick me up and meet my parents.

'So, were they OK about the fact that I'm not Greek?' he asks me after I've told him about it.

'Eventually,' I reply. I explain to him that I have a feeling that my mum thinks that Persian is almost Greek anyway!'

* * *

'So, Nima, what do you want to study when you finish taking you're A-levels?' my dad asks, after shaking Nima's hand and offering him a seat. He is being so embarrassing! Anyone would think that the poor boy has come to ask for my hand in marriage – not just to take me to a bonfire party!

'Well, I haven't decided yet,' poor Nima replies politely, 'I like architecture, but I haven't made my mind up.'

My mum, after bringing a tray piled with Greek sweets, coffee for my brother and father and Cokes for me and Nima, sits opposite him and wears a silly smile throughout the entire conversation, understanding nothing of what is being said. My brother, on the other hand, looks suspiciously at Nima from across the room, but thankfully lets my father do the talking.

Dad continues with the cross-examination. 'And your father? What business is he in?'

'He's an architect,' Nima replies.

'Oh, very good! Does he have his own business?' Dad asks with great interest. Business is of paramount importance to Greeks.

'Yes he does,' Nima says patiently.

'So, you can go and work with him if you decide to become an architect.'

'Oh, look at the time!' I interrupt jumping up and looking at my watch. Enough is enough, I decide. It's time we left for the party.

'I'm so sorry,' I tell him once we're out of the house. 'They're just impossible!'

'Honestly, Julia,' he says, taking my hand, 'my parents are just the same. I saw this so many times with my dad when my sister first brought boys home. It's just funny being on the receiving end this time.'

The party is only a bus ride away, in a big house on top of the hill.

'I've known Charlie since junior school,' he tells me as we get to the front door, 'and although he's at a different school now, we're still friends.'

'Most of my friends in Cyprus are people I've known since junior school,' I say, 'but I haven't seen any of them for over a year now.'

Charlie's house isn't attached to any other houses and has a huge garden all the way around. His parents are in the kitchen while all the kids are building a bonfire in the back.

'Is it allowed to have fires in gardens?' I ask Nima. 'Isn't it dangerous?'

'Not if you know what you're doing,' he says. 'Don't worry, as long as some adults are here, it's fine. That's why his parents have stayed – to keep an eye on things.'

It's a clear night and, standing in the garden at the top of the hill, there is a spectacular view of the city. London is sprawled out in front of us, a myriad lights sparkling at our feet.

'We'll have the most amazing view of all the fireworks across London from here,' Nima tells me and I can't wait to see them for the first time.

Some of the kids are standing around the fire which is now burning, and others are sitting on the grass all around the garden. The glow of the flames light up and warm our faces and some people are wrapping potatoes in silver foil and placing them on the edge of the fire.

'Why are they doing that?' I ask Nima with curiosity.

'They're making baked potatoes,' he explains. 'They cook slowly and then when they are cooked through, you unwrap them, cut them open and put butter in the middle. You never tasted anything so delicious! The best way to eat potatoes – just wait and see.'

Charlie and his dad and a few adults are setting up fireworks all around the garden, and Nima decides to go and help them. 'Will you be OK on your own for a bit?' he asks.

I'm happy to stand in the warm glow of the fire, listening to the chatter around me and drifting into a contented trance. Spellbound, I watch the dancing flames flickering, licking the burning wood. Suddenly I'm shaken out of my trance by a series of ear-bursting bangs, explosions and blinding flashes that send me into a spin of panic and fear. With my heart pounding so fast it feels like it's going to burst, I let out a blood-curdling scream that stops everyone around me dead in their tracks.

In a split second, Nima is by my side. 'What's wrong?' he says in a panic, wrapping his arms around me very tight, while everyone else stands and stares at me. 'Are you hurt?' He searches me to see if I was hit by a firework. Charlie's parents have run to see what's happened and they want to take me inside the house. Shaking, I cling to Nima and burst into tears.

CHAPTER THIRTY-ONE

Emotional Download

Sitting on the sofa with Nima in the warm living room, cradling a cup of tea in my hands, I try to explain what triggered my reaction. 'I'm so sorry,' I whisper to him, feeling very embarrassed. 'I just panicked. I thought it was a bomb.'

'Why did you think *that*?' He is looking at me with a puzzled expression.

'I've never seen fireworks like these before. They were so loud and so close, and there seemed to be so many explosions one after the other – it really scared me,' I explain and seeing his worried frown, I realise that I will have to try to explain to him where it all came from.

'I don't really talk about it much,' I begin. 'I don't know if you know, but three years ago there was a war in my country and we were all caught up in it.'

'Did you see actual bombs and fighting?' he asks, his expression becoming even more serious than before and his voice even more concerned.

'Yes. Bombs, guns, dead bodies . . . everything,' I tell him in a whisper, fighting back tears. 'It was summer. You can't imagine the heat in my country in July. The Turkish army invaded at five in the morning when we were all asleep, apart from my mum, who was watering the garden in her nightie. She looked up and she saw hundreds of parachutes dropping out of the sky. She woke us up and we had to get in the car, still in our pyjamas, and my dad drove like mad to get away from our house, because it was really close to the fighting.'

'Where did you go?' Nima asks gently taking my hand.

'To begin with, my father started to drive towards the mountains, but the roads looked too dangerous, so he turned back and we went to my uncle's house in Nicosia – they have a basement garage there, deep down under their apartment block. Because of the basement, they thought it was safe from the bombs, and when we got there, it was full of other people – everyone had had the same idea. Lots of relatives were there and some friends and neighbours. Everybody kept piling in and of course my uncle took everyone in. My cousin Sophia and I just huddled up together in a corner listening to the fighting outside, and we all stayed there for three days and three nights while bombs dropped around us. My really little cousins didn't understand and thought it was an adventure, but you can't imagine how scared we were and how hot and airless it was in that basement.'

'Did you have any food?' I feel Nima's grip on my hand tighten.

'At times when the bombing stopped some of the adults would go to the apartments upstairs and grab some food and water, and bedding to sleep on. We just put some sheets down and slept on the concrete floor. The bombing seemed to happen in waves and when there was a break we could also sneak upstairs to go to the loo. My dad said it was when the planes went to refuel. It was really scary because there was still gunfire, and bullets bouncing off the buildings, so we had to crawl on the ground, away from the windows. We could hear the adults making plans and they decided that as soon as we could, we should try to get up to the mountains to my grandfather's village. Then one day when it all seemed to go quiet we made a run for it. We piled as many people as we could in the cars and headed for the mountains – through the fields most of the time because the roads were closed. We saw hundreds of cars and trucks full of other people, some with their belongings piled on top of their cars, also heading for the mountains. At one point, we got stuck behind a truck full of people all lying down together. They were women and children and old men. They seemed to be asleep, and I asked my dad what they were doing, but before he could answer, I realised that they were all dead.'

My voice is almost a whisper now and tears are rolling down my cheeks. Nima takes both of my hands into his and holds them tight.

'We stayed at my grandfather's village for a month with hundreds of other people like us, sleeping all over the place – in fields, in churches, under trees . . . everywhere. We were twenty-five people in his little two-bedroomed house. My grandfather had to sleep in the bath. There were no bombs or gunfire in the mountains, but some people were scared that the fighting would spread there too . . . In fact, one day a big row broke between the men, because one of them decided we needed something to protect ourselves in case we were attacked. He got this massive butcher's knife and put it right in the middle of the kitchen table. My dad and uncle went mad telling him that he had to get rid of it because far from protecting us, we were more likely to be killed by it. In the end, we had to put it to a vote and everyone thought it was a stupid idea and so he got rid of it.'

'So what happened – how did it all end?'

'Well, after the war finished, Cyprus was partitioned. The island got divided into two parts, north and south, and the Turkish people had to go and live in the north and we stayed in the south,' I explain. 'But the trouble was, if you were Greek and lived in the north you had to leave everything behind and come and live in the south and the same with the Turkish people; they had to do the opposite.'

'But you lived in the south, right? So you were OK?' he asks. 'Did you know anyone who had to leave their homes behind?' he asks.

'Yes, lots of people. You know my friend Anna I told you about that we used to live with – her family had to leave everything behind. That's why they came to live in England. Some people even got killed when they were trying to escape. And my mum's best friend who's Turkish and lived near us, she had to go to the north and we never see her or her family any more. It's really sad for everyone.'

'But why did it all happen?' Nima asks, trying to make sense of what I'm telling him.

'Oh God, Nima, I don't know exactly. It goes back such a long time; I don't quite understand it myself . . . lots of reasons, I suppose. It's all too difficult to explain. All I know is that it's all such a mess and no one is happy.'

'What would you like to do now?' he asks finally, leaning over to give me a little kiss. 'Do you want me to take you home?

'No, I'm fine now,' I tell him, wiping my eyes and standing up. 'Lets go outside and see what's happening. I'd like to see some fireworks if there are any left. I'm so sorry, Nima. I hope your friends don't think I'm completely mad,' I say, managing a little smile.

Out in the cool air, the bonfire is still ablaze, and although the party fireworks had long burned out, the London night sky is lit up by hundreds of other displays. Standing in a garden high on a hill, holding Nima's hand, with the city sprawled in front of us, I am no longer frightened and I witness the most spectacular fireworks I have ever seen. I watch the black night light up in a kaleidoscope of colours, enchanted. They explode one after the other, rising and falling like a fountain of multi-coloured jewels trickling into the city, and with each one we all let out a cheer of approval. Out of the corner of my eye, I notice a discarded box on the table that I'm leaning on, with the word 'Pyrotechnics' written on it. I smile to myself and think, 'pyro' from the Greek word for 'fire' and 'technics' from the Greek word for 'art'! In other words, *art* with *fire*. I can't get away from Greek! I think, and smile.

CHAPTER THIRTY-TWO

Coming Clean

'I can't tell you what a fool I felt,' I tell Anna, and blush just thinking about it. We are waiting for Peter and Tom to meet us in a café the following Saturday. 'Every-one was having fun, it was all lovely, and then I let out a scream like someone was stabbing me. It was *so* embarrassing, and I gave everyone, including myself, such a fright.'

'I completely understand. I'd have probably done the same,' Anna says, because if anyone is going to understand how I felt at that moment, she would.

'It was so weird, Anna. I couldn't believe that after all this time something like fireworks would trigger such a strong reaction in me. I was just so surprised by it. Do you think we will ever forget all that stuff?'

'Oh God, Ioulia, how can we? I think about it such a lot – usually when I'm lying in bed at night. That's when things flash through my head. I honestly don't think it's something we can ever forget.'

'I understand lying in bed in the dark and being haunted by things I've seen, but this was different,' I tell her. 'I really didn't expect to freak out like that at a party when I was feeling so relaxed and happy.'

'It's all in our subconscious, Ioulia *mou*, and maybe people like us who've been through a war will always carry that with them.'

'I suppose you're right,' I say and take a sip of my cappuccino. 'Still, the good thing that's come out of it is that now I've told someone, and Nima is the right person.' Anna and I often share our feelings and experiences about the war, but it isn't something we particularly want to dwell on, or talk about much with other people. But I suppose my war experience is such a big part of who I am, and telling Nima has brought me closer to him.

'You obviously really like Nima,' Anna says, smiling. 'I think you've made the right decision to talk to Tom.'

Even though I've been seeing a lot of Nima since September and getting a lot closer to him, I've still kept up my friendship with Tom. He's so talented and clever, and I enjoy talking about art with him. I know I could learn a lot from him, but I also know he's wrong for me and that it's wrong for me to be stringing him along. So, finally, after a particularly long phone call in which Tom was trying his best to convince me to go out with him, I've decided to tell him I'm seeing someone else.

I feel sick to my stomach with nerves. I'm nervous about seeing Tom again, I'm nervous about ending it with him and I'm nervous about doing something I've never done before; it all feels very grown-up and I don't like it one bit. The rain is pelting down hard outside, as we wait for the two boys to arrive.

'I think I should talk to him on my own,' I tell Anna.

She nods. 'Don't worry, we'll go for a walk and leave you to talk.' Anna is always pleased to see Peter, and going off alone with him is no hardship.

When we're halfway through our second cappuccino, Tom and Peter walk into the steamed-up café, dripping wet and frozen. Anna jumps up and, grabbing her bag, she leads Peter back out into the pouring rain.

'How have you been, Julia?' Tom asks, sitting down opposite me and cupping my mug of coffee with both his hands to warm them up. He flashes me one of his dazzling smiles.

Looking into his blue eyes and handsome face, I get all stirred up and confused about my feelings again. Why can't I have two boyfriends? I think, and then instantly recall the night of Stella's party, being on the bed with him amongst the coats, and I know that this boy is way ahead of me. Suddenly the contrast between Tom and Nima is very clear. Tom is a man – he's not a boy. He's a man ready for a relationship with an equal; he could have a *kid*, for God's sake. I'm not ready for a grown-up boyfriend yet!

Nima, on the other hand, is a boy and he's going through the same things as I am. With him, I always feel comfortable and relaxed. I can be myself. I can't be myself with Tom.

'Oh, fine . . .' I reply, feeling tongue-tied.

'I'm really glad you wanted to see me at last,' Tom says, still smiling. 'You know how much I like you, Julia.'

That comment makes me feel sick. 'I know, Tom.

That's why I wanted to see you. I wanted to tell you that I've started seeing someone else.'

'Oh . . .' he says and suddenly the smile disappears from his face. 'Is he Greek?'

'No, actually, he's Iranian,' I reply, and looking at his face I feel even worse than before.

'And how long have you been seeing him – is it serious?'

'Just a couple of months. I don't know what you mean by serious – he's just a boy I'm going out with.'

'Well, if he's just a boy you're going out with, why can't you go out with me too?' he asks, staring straight into my eyes.

'Well . . . I don't know,' I say, feeling confused. 'I don't think that would work.'

'Why not?' he insists. 'We really like each other and we have a lot in common. Let's give it a chance and see where it goes.'

'No, I don't think it would work,' I say again. I can't think how else to explain to him that it wouldn't go anywhere – or at least, because of what happened on the bed at the party, not where he wants it to go.

'I think it *could* work,' he persists, smiling again, and I suddenly realise there's only one way he'll ever understand what I'm trying to say to him.

'Tom,' I hear myself say, 'I'm fifteen years old!'

'*What?*' he says, leaning back in his chair with a sudden jerk and knocking my empty cup over. His gaze seems to stay fixed on me for an eternity. 'I didn't know . . . you look much older . . . I thought you were at least the same age as Anna.'

CHAPTER THIRTY-THREE

Torn

'You should have seen his face, Anna,' I tell her as we walk home in the rain, huddled up together under one umbrella. 'He was really shocked. I knew he'd be surprised, but I didn't realise he'd be *that* surprised.'

'You had to tell him,' replies Anna. 'You had to tell him how old you are – otherwise he would never have given up.'

'I did feel sorry for him . . . but I also feel so much better about everything now. What are you going to do about Peter?' I ask her. 'Will you carry on seeing him?'

'I don't see why not. We get on fine.'

'Do you think you'll tell your parents about him?'

'No point in doing that just yet,' she says thoughtfully. 'I don't know what's going to happen when I go to university. I can't face all the drama of explaining it to them if it's going to be for nothing . . . I'll see.'

'I'm really happy I told my mum about Nima,' I tell her. 'It just makes it so much easier not having to sneak around all the time.'

'You're right,' she says. 'It *is* better, and I might still do it, but I just want to see where it goes first.'

* * *

'Where have *you* two been?' asks Tony as we walk through the front door like a couple of drowned rats.

'We went out for a coffee,' I say. 'Where are you going?'

'That's none of your business,' he snaps, grabbing Dad's car keys and dashing out, leaving a waft of aftershave behind him.

'I think he's got a girlfriend,' Mum says to us with a little smile and a nod after he's gone. 'A girl called him earlier and he was on the phone for hours, and,' she adds in amazement, 'he spent ages getting ready!'

'Most unlike Tony,' I say.

'Well!' says Anna, folding her arms and raising her eyebrows.

'It must be *some* girl!' I add with a big grin.

'Or should you say *woman*?' Anna says, and we all start laughing.

'What does your family do for Christmas?' Nima asks me a couple of days later when we're on the bus.

'Just the usual stuff – big turkey lunch and things,' I reply. 'We spend it with my friend Anna's family. But we've only ever had one Christmas here, last year with all that snow – the snow was great!'

'What are you going to do this year?'

'I'm going to Cyprus,' I reply.

'Just you?' he says, sounding surprised.

'My dad said I can go and spend it with my cousin Sophia.'

'Will you be away for the whole holiday?'

'My parents said I can go as soon as school finishes and stay till the New Year.'

'Oh, that's a shame,' he says with disappointment in his voice. 'I was thinking of having a New Year's Eve party and I wanted you to be there.'

'Oh, really?' I say, suddenly feeling strangely torn. 'New Year's Eve is such a big celebration in Cyprus . . .' I carry on. 'We make more fuss about it than Christmas – and I know my aunt and uncle will be having a party.'

'Oh well, that's a shame,' he says again. 'I thought it would be good to have a party and you could have sort of helped me . . .' His voice trails off.

'Oh, Nima, I'd really have loved that, but what can I do if I'm going away?'

'I don't know why, but I thought you'd be here,' he says. 'What with it being Christmas and everything . . . I thought you'd be here with your family.'

'My family is there too, and I miss them and Cyprus so much – can you have a party another time?' I ask hopefully.

'I'll have to ask my mum,' he says. 'My parents are going out on New Year's Eve and it seemed like a good idea to have it then.'

'Sorry, Nima,' I say, and sit a bit closer, linking my arm through his.

All through dinner, my mind keeps going back to the conversation about the party. I feel really confused about my feelings. Up until then I was deliriously happy at the thought of my Christmas trip. I couldn't wait to see everyone again and do all the things I'd planned with

Sophia. But now, for the first time, I feel a cloud hovering over the idea.

'So, how come *she* gets to have a Christmas holiday and I have to wait till summer?' Tony complains while we eat.

'You can go too, if you really want to,' Mum tells him. 'I thought you were quite happy to stay here with all your friends and all those parties you've been invited to.'

'I am really. I was just teasing her. London's great at Christmas and I'd rather wait for the summer to go to Cyprus,' he says with a smile, taking another slice of mousaka.

'Have some more food, Ioulia,' Mum says, handing me the salad bowl.

'No, thanks,' I reply, taking it and putting it down again without having any more.

'What's the matter, Ioulia *mou*? You haven't eaten much . . .' Mum asks, looking worried. 'Do you feel all right?'

'I'm not very hungry, Mama. I'm just really tired. I think I'll go to bed,' I say and leave the table.

CHAPTER THIRTY-FOUR

Decision Time

'What's wrong?' Linda asks as we try to eat a particularly disgusting school lunch of liver, onions and lumpy mashed potatoes. 'You look like you haven't slept all night!'

'I didn't much,' I reply, yawning. 'I lay in bed most of the night thinking. I can't keep my eyes open now.'

'Thinking about what?'

'Oh God, I just don't know what to do. You know I'm supposed to be going to Cyprus for Christmas . . .'

'What do you mean "supposed to be going"?' she interrupts. 'You *are* going, aren't you?' She gives me a raised-eyebrow look.

'Well, the problem is, Nima told me yesterday that he wants to have a New Year's Eve party and he *really* wants me to be there – and the trouble is, Linda, I *really* want to be there too!'

'More than going to Cyprus?' she asks, her voice rising, and looking like her eyes are about to pop out of her head.

'That's the thing. I think I do . . . and I can't quite believe it . . .' I say, my voice trailing off.

'What about Sophia? Won't she be really disappointed? I can't believe this! All you've talked about since she left is Christmas!'

'I know! That's the weird thing about it. Going to Cyprus has been the one thing I've wanted ever since I came here and now that I'm supposed to be going in a couple of weeks, I'm having second thoughts . . . I don't know what's happened to me.'

'That's it, I knew it!' she says, putting down her knife and fork and staring at me. 'You're in love! That's what's happened to you. You've got it bad, girl!'

'It's not just that!' I protest, 'I do really like Nima, but it's also that I just don't want to miss out on all the fun here. Last year I didn't know anyone, but now it's all so different . . . There's you and Anna and Stella, who's thinking of having a Christmas party, and Nima. Even one of my brother's friends has invited me to a party – not that Tony will let me go, of course, but still . . .' I can't quite believe what I am saying. It's amazing how much has happened to me in just over a year. I'm still the same, but I feel almost like a different person, sitting there in the school dining hall, talking with Linda and surrounded by the buzz of girlie chatter. I feel totally grounded, like I belong. Everything is familiar, in contrast to a year ago when I felt displaced and alien, hearing nothing and understanding nothing, shrouded in a miserable, grey cloud.

'So, what are you going to do?' asks Linda, bringing me out of my thoughts.

'I think I'd better talk to my parents,' I say, as we get up to leave the table.

* * *

'Can I talk to you please, Mama?' I ask as soon as I get home from school. My mum is sitting at her sewing machine – one of the first things she bought when we moved into our flat – making herself a dress. She always loved making clothes when we lived in Cyprus, so it's great that she's able to do it again.

Mum puts down the ruby-red velvet cloth she is working with and looks over her glasses and smiles at me.

'Of course, Ioulia *mou*. What's on your mind?'

'It's about going to Cyprus at Christmas, Mama,' I say quietly.

'Yes . . . what about it? You can go as soon as the school is finished and not before,' she says a little sternly, assuming that I'm just getting impatient to go.

'I know, but it's not that . . . I just wanted to know if you've already bought my ticket.'

'I think your father is getting it next week,' she says. 'Why do you ask?

'What would you say if I told you I'm not sure I want to go?' I say looking at her face to gauge her reaction.

She takes her glasses off and gives me a puzzled and worried look. 'Why wouldn't you want to go? What's the matter? Are you all right?'

'I'm absolutely fine, Mama,' I say. Of course my mother would think that something was terribly wrong with me when I've asked such an unlikely question. 'It's just that I was thinking that since we're all going to Cyprus in the summer, I don't need to go for Christmas as well . . .'

165

'But we thought you were so homesick and you really wanted to go . . .' she says, confused.

'Well, I was, and I'm really grateful, but everything is so different now. I feel so much better since I saw Sophia this summer, and there is *so* much happening in London at Christmas, and Nima is having a party and I don't want to miss it . . .' I tell her without stopping to take a breath.

'Oh . . .' she says. 'That's all right, no problem, it's fine . . . don't go. If you'd rather stay, so much the better – we can all be together for Christmas.'

'You don't mind?' I say, and let out a big sigh of relief.

'Why should I mind? We were doing it for you.' She gives me another smile and strokes my cheek. 'I suppose Sophia might be a bit disappointed, so you better let her know.'

'I will Mama, I will,' I say with a big smile and give her a hug and a kiss. But I know Sophia will be fine. She always understands me, and besides, we'll be together the whole summer next year. 'You know what?' I add. 'I didn't have any idea what to do about this and I was thinking of asking *Kyria* Eva to read my coffee cup for some clues, but there's no need. I just know I'd rather stay.'